No one writes romantic fiction like Barbara Cartland.

Miss Cartland was originally inspired by the best of the romantic novelists she read as a girl—Elinor Glyn, Ethel M. Dell, Ian Hay and E. M. Hull. Convinced that her own wide audience would also delight in her favorite authors, Barbara Cartland has taken their classic tales of romance and specially adapted them for today's readers.

Bantam is proud to publish these novels—personally selected and edited by Miss Cartland—under the imprint

**BARBARA CARTLAND'S
LIBRARY OF LOVE**

Bantam Books by Barbara Cartland
Ask your bookseller for the books you have missed

1 THE DARING DECEPTION
3 THE LITTLE ADVENTURE
4 LESSONS IN LOVE
6 THE BORED BRIDEGROOM
7 THE PENNILESS PEER
8 THE DANGEROUS DANDY
9 THE RUTHLESS RAKE
10 THE WICKED MARQUIS
11 THE CASTLE OF FEAR
12 THE GLITTERING LIGHTS
13 A SWORD TO THE HEART
14 THE KARMA OF LOVE
16 BEWITCHED
18 THE FRIGHTENED BRIDE
19 THE SHADOW OF SIN
21 THE TEARS OF LOVE
22 A VERY NAUGHTY
    ANGEL
23 CALL OF THE HEART
24 THE DEVIL IN LOVE
25 AS EAGLES FLY
26 LOVE IS INNOCENT
27 SAY YES, SAMANTHA
28 THE CRUEL COUNT
29 THE MASK OF LOVE
30 FIRE ON THE SNOW
31 AN ARROW OF LOVE
32 A GAMBLE WITH
    HEARTS
33 A KISS FOR THE KING
34 A FRAME OF DREAMS
35 THE FRAGRANT FLOWER
36 THE ELUSIVE EARL
37 MOON OVER EDEN
38 THE GOLDEN ILLUSION
39 THE HUSBAND HUNTERS
41 PASSIONS IN THE SAND
42 THE SLAVES OF LOVE
43 AN ANGEL IN HELL
44 THE WILD CRY OF LOVE
45 THE BLUE-EYED WITCH
46 THE INCREDIBLE
    HONEYMOON
47 A DREAM FROM THE
    NIGHT
48 CONQUERED BY LOVE
49 NEVER LAUGH AT LOVE
50 THE SECRET OF THE
    GLEN
51 THE PROUD PRINCESS
52 HUNGRY FOR LOVE
53 THE HEART TRIUMPHANT
54 THE DREAM AND THE
    GLORY
55 THE TAMING OF LADY
    LORINDA
56 THE DISGRACEFUL DUKE
57 VOTE FOR LOVE
58 THE MYSTERIOUS MAID-
    SERVANT
59 THE MAGIC OF LOVE
60 KISS THE MOONLIGHT
61 A RHAPSODY OF LOVE
62 THE MARQUIS WHO
    HATED WOMEN
63 LOOK, LISTEN AND LOVE
64 A DUEL WITH DESTINY
65 THE CURSE OF THE CLAN
66 PUNISHMENT OF A VIXEN
67 THE OUTRAGEOUS LADY

Barbara Cartland's Library of Love

1 THE SHEIK
2 HIS HOUR
3 THE KNAVE OF DIAMONDS
4 A SAFETY MATCH
5 THE HUNDREDTH CHANCE
6 THE REASON WHY

Barbara Cartland's Library of Love

THE REASON WHY
BY ELINOR GLYN
CONDENSED
BY BARBARA CARTLAND

BANTAM BOOKS · TORONTO · NEW YORK · LONDON

THE REASON WHY
A Bantam Book / July 1977

ISBN 0-553-10926-X

Published simultaneously in the United States and Canada

Bantam Books are published by Bantam Books, Inc. Its trade-
mark, consisting of the words "Bantam Books" and the por-
trayal of a bantam, is registered in the United States Patent
Office and in other countries. Marca Registrada. Bantam
Books, Inc., 666 Fifth Avenue, New York, New York 10019.

PRINTED IN THE UNITED STATES OF AMERICA

Introduction
by
Barbara Cartland

This is one of Elinor Glyn's most passionate and moving stories. No one could resist the handsome, self-controlled Lord Tancred or the beautiful, proud, resentful Zara with her red hair and deeply hidden emotions.

Add the frail figure of her delicate little brother, the hard, wealthy, manipulating financier who is her uncle, and a secret which baffles, misleads, and tantalises the hero so that tragedy is only averted by a hair's breadth.

What more could anyone ask?

The
Reason
Why

Chapter
One

People sometimes wondered from what nation the great financier Francis Markrute originally sprang.

Now a naturalised Englishman, he looked unobtrusively English, being slight, fair, and aged about forty-six.

No one knew anything about him, except that he was fabulously rich and had descended upon London some ten years previously.

As he sat smoking a fine cigar in his library, which looked out on the park, a young man lounged in a great leather chair opposite to him.

There was no doubt about this visitor's nationality! He was flamboyantly English. He was, perhaps, more Norman than Saxon, for his hair was dark, though his eyes were blue.

Francis Markrute always smoked his cigars to the end, but Lord Tancred (Tristram Lorrimer Guiscard Guiscard, twenty-fourth Baron Tancred, or Wrayth in the County of Suffolk) usually absent-

1

mindedly flung his into the grate after a few whiffs.

He did so now, and he laughed with a slightly whimsical bitterness as he went on with the conversation.

"Yes, Francis, my friend, I am thirty, and there is nothing interesting left for me to do but to emigrate to Canada and take up a ranch."

"Wrayth mortgaged heavily, I suppose?" said Mr Markrute, quietly.

"Pretty badly."

The financier half-closed his eyes. When he did this, there was always something of importance working in his brain.

"You have not any glaring vices, Tancred," he said. "You are no gambler, either on the turf or at cards. You are not over-addicted to expensive ladies. You are cultivated, for a sportsman.

"You are, in fact, rather a fine specimen of your class. It seems a pity you should have to shut down and go to the colonies."

"Oh, I don't know! And I have not altogether got to shut down," Tancred replied, "only the show is growing rather rotten over here. We have let the rabble, the most unfit and ignorant, have this casting vote, and the machine now will crush any man. I have kept out of politics as much as I can, and I am glad."

"I have a proposition to make to you, should you care to accept it," Francis Markrute said slowly. "I have a niece, a widow, she is rather an

2

attractive lady. If you will marry her, I will pay off all your mortgages, and settle on her quite a princely dower."

"Good God!" said Lord Tancred.

The financier's eyes for an instant gave forth a flash of steel.

There had been an infinite variety of meanings hidden in the exclamation, but he demanded suavely:

"What point of the question causes you to exclaim 'Good God'?"

"The whole thing," Lord Tancred replied; "to marry at all to begin with, and to marry an unknown woman, to have one's debts paid for the rest, it is a tall order."

"A most common occurrence. Think of the number of your peers who have gone to America for their wives, for no other reason."

"And think of the rotters they are, most of them!" Lord Tancred answered. "I mayn't be much catch financially, but I have one of the oldest names and titles in England, and up to now we have not had any cads or cowards in the family."

He paused before he continued.

"By Jove! Francis, what are you driving at? Confound it, man, I am not starving, and can work if it should ever come to that."

Mr Markrute smoothed his hands.

"Yes, it was a blunder, I admit, to put it this way. So I will be frank with you. My family is also,

3

my friend, as old as yours. My niece is all I have left in the world. I would like to see her married to an Englishman.

"I would like to see her married to you of all Englishmen, because I like you, and you have qualities about you which count in life. Oh, believe me . . ."

He raised a protesting finger to quell an interruption.

"I have studied you these years, there is nothing you can say of yourself or your affairs that I do not know."

"My dear old boy," Lord Tancred laughed, "we have been friends for a long time, and now we are coming to home truths. I must say I like your deuced cold-blooded point of view on every subject.

"I like your knowledge of wine and cigars and pictures, and you are a most entertaining companion. But 'pon my soul, I should not like to have your niece for a wife, if she takes after you!"

"You think she would be cold-blooded, too?"

"Undoubtedly, but it is all perfectly preposterous. I don't believe you mean a word you are saying, it is some kind of a joke!"

"Have you ever known me to make such jokes, Tancred?" Mr Markrute asked calmly.

"No, I haven't, and that is the odd part of it. What the devil do you mean?"

"I mean what I say, I will pay every debt you

have, and give you a charming wife with a fortune."

Lord Tancred got up and walked about the room.

"It is nonsense, Francis, I could not do it; I have, as you know, knocked about the world, and since you are aware of everything about me, you have probably heard of some of my likes, and dislikes.

"I never run after a woman unless she attracts me, and I would never marry unless I were madly in love. What is more, I believe I should hate a wife with money."

"You would marry a woman, then, if you were in love?" Francis Markrute asked.

"Probably, but I have never been really in love, have you? It is all story-book stuff, that Almighty passion, I expect."

"I have understood it is possible for a woman to matter," the financier said, and he drew in his lips.

"Well, up to now I have not," Lord Tancred announced, "and may the day be far off when I shall. I feel pretty safe!"

A strange mysterious smile crept over Mr Markrute's face.

"By the way, how do you know the lady would be willing to marry me, Francis? You spoke as if I were the only person to be consulted in the affair."

"So you are. I can answer for my niece; she will do as I wish, and, as I said before, you are rather a perfect picture of an English nobleman, Tancred."

" 'Pon my word, it is amusing," he laughed, "your turning into a sort of matrimonial agent; can't you see the fun of the thing yourself?"

"It seems quite natural to me. You have every social advantage to offer a woman, and a presentable person, and my niece has youth, and some looks, and a large fortune.

"But we will say no more about it. I shall be glad to be of any service I can to you, anyway, with regard to your Canadian scheme. Come and dine tonight. I happen to have asked a couple of railway magnates with interests out there, and you can get some information from them."

Lord Tancred agreed and got up to go, but just at the door he paused and said with a laugh:

"And shall I see the niece?"

The financier had his back turned, and so he permitted the flicker of a smile to come over his mouth as he answered:

"It might be, but we have dismissed the subject of the niece."

At the sound of the closing of the door, Mr Markrute pressed a button which lay on his writing-table, and a servant entered the room.

"Tell the Countess Shulski I wish to speak to her immediately," he said. "Ask her to come at once."

6

But he had to walk up and down several times, and was growing impatient, before the door opened and a woman came slowly into the room.

The financier paused in his restless pacing as he heard the door open, and stood perfectly still with his back to the light.

The woman advanced, and also stood still, and they looked at each other, with no great love in their eyes.

She was rather tall and very slender, and yet in every voluptuous curve of her lithe body she refuted the idea of thinness.

Her head was small, her face small and oval, and her skin something quite exceptional in its white purity, not the purity of milk but the purity of rich white velvet or the petal of a gardenia.

Her mouth was curved and red and her teeth were very even. When she smiled, they suggested something of great strength, though they were small and white.

Her two wonders were her eyes and her hair. At first you could have sworn the eyes were black, just great pools of ink, or discs of black velvet set in their broad lids, and shaded with jet lashes.

But if they chanced to glance up in the full light then you knew they were slate colour, not a tinge of brown or green, the whole iris a uniform shade.

Strange slumbrous resentful eyes, under straight thick black brows, the expression full of all sorts of meanings, though none of them peaceful or calm. And from some far-back Spanish ancestress she probably got that glorious head of red hair, the colour of a ripe chestnut when it falls from its shell, or a beautifully groomed bright bay horse.

The heavy plaits, which were wound tightly round her head, must have fallen below her knees when they were undone. Her coiffure gave the impression that she never thought of fashion, or changed its form of dressing from year to year.

But it was the exquisite plaiting of the hair on her forehead, as it waved back in broad waves, that made up the perfection and Greek simplicity of the whole thing. Nothing about her had been aided by conscious art.

Her black dress was rather poor, though she wore it with the traditional air of an empress. Indeed, she looked an empress, from the tips of her perfect fingers to her small arched feet.

"Well . . . what is it? Why have you sent for me so peremptorily?" she asked in a low cultured voice.

"I asked you to come down to discuss a matter of great importance. Will you be good enough to be seated?" he said.

He drew forward a chair, into which she sank, and there waited with folded hands for him to continue.

Her stillness was always as intent as his own, but whereas his had a nervous tension of conscious repression, hers had an unconscious quiet force. Her father had been an Englishman, but both uncle and niece at moments made people feel they were silent panthers, ready to spring.

"You are in a miserable position," Francis Markrute said, "hardly enough to eat at times, as I understand. When I sent for you from Paris last week, I expect you guessed that I had some plan in my head."

"Naturally," she said, with fine contempt. "I did not mistake it for kindness!"

"Then it is well, and we can come to the point," he said. "I am sorry that I have had to be away since your arrival until yesterday. I trust my servants have made you comfortable?"

"Quite comfortable," she answered coldly.

"Good! You have no doubt, I suppose, that your husband, Count Ladislaus Shulski, is dead? There is no possible mistake in his identity? I believe his face was practically shot away."

Francis Markrute paused before he continued.

"I have taken the precaution to inform myself upon every point from the authorities at Monte Carlo, but I wish for your final testimony."

"Ladislaus Shulski is dead," his niece replied quietly, but in a tone as though it gave her pleasure to say it. "The woman Feto caused the fray, Ivan Larski shot him in her arms, he was her lover.

"She wailed over the body like an animal bereaved of its young. She was there lamenting his

9

fine eyes when they sent for me! They were gone forever, but no one could mistake his curly hair, or his cruel white hands."

She shivered.

"Ah! It was a scene of disgust; I have witnessed many ugly things, but that was of the worst. I do not wish to talk of it, it was all over a year ago."

"And since then you have lived from hand to mouth, with those others."

Francis Markrute's voice took on a new shade, there was a cold hate in it.

"I have lived with my little brother, Mirko, and Mimo, how could I desert them? Sometimes we have found it hard at the end of the quarter; but it was not always as bad as that, especially when Mimo sold a picture. . . ."

"I will not hear his name!" Francis Markrute said, with some excitement. "In the beginning, if I could have found him I would have killed him, as you know, but now since my sister is dead, he is not worth powder and shot!"

The Countess Shulski gave the faintest shrug of her shoulders, while her eyes grew blacker with resentment. She did not speak.

Francis Markrute stood by the mantelpiece and lit a cigar before he continued, and he knew he must choose his words.

"You are twenty-three years old, Zara, and you were married at sixteen," he said at last. "And up to thirteen, at least, I know you were very highly educated. You understand something of life, I expect."

"Life!" she said.

There was a concentrated essence of bitterness in her voice.

"*Mon Dieu!* . . . Life . . . and men!"

"Yes, you probably think you know men."

She lifted her upper lip a little, and showed her even teeth.

"I know that they are either selfish weaklings, cruel, hateful brutes like Ladislaus, or clever, successful financiers, like you, that is enough! We women must always be sacrificed."

"Well, you don't know Englishmen."

"Yes, I remember my father very well. Cold and hard to my darling . . ."

Her voice trembled a little.

"He only thought of himself, to rush to England for support, and leave her alone for months and months. Selfish and vile, all of them!"

"In spite of that, I have found you an English husband, whom you will be good enough to take, Madame," Francis Markrute announced authoritatively.

She gave a little laugh, if anything so mirthless could be called a laugh.

"I think you will," the financier said, with quiet assurance, "if I know you. There are terms, of course."

She glanced at him sharply, the expression in those sombre eyes was often alert like those of a wild animal about to be attacked, only she had trained herself generally to keep the lids lowered.

"What are the terms?" she asked.

As she spoke, Francis Markrute thought of the black panther in the Zoo, whom he was so fond of going to watch on Sunday mornings.

He had been constrained up to this, but now the question being one of business, all his natural ease of manner returned, and he sat down opposite her.

"The terms are that the boy Mirko, your half-brother, shall be provided for for life. He shall live with decent people, and have his talent properly cultivated."

He stopped abruptly and remained silent.

"Ah, God!" she said, so low he could only just hear her. "I have paid the price of my body and soul once for them. It is too much to ask it of me a second time. . . ."

"That is as you please," said the financier.

He seldom made a mistake in his methods with people. He left nothing to chance; he led the conversation up to the right point, fired his bomb, and then showed absolute indifference.

He left his niece in silence, while she pondered over his bargain, knowing full well what would be the result. She got up from her chair and leaned upon the back of it, while her face looked white as death in the dying afternoon's light.

"Can you realise what my life was like with

Ladislaus?" she hissed. "A plaything for his brutal pleasures to begin with, later a decoy duck to trap the other men. I hated him always, but he seemed so kind beforehand, kind to my darling mother, whom you were leaving to die."

Francis Markrute winced, and a look of pain came into his hard face, as his niece went on.

"And she was beginning to be ill even at that time, and we were so poor, so I married him."

Then she swept towards the door with her empress air, and as she got there she turned and spoke again.

"I tell you it is too much," she said, with almost a sob in her voice. "I will not do it. . . ."

She went out and closed the door.

Francis Markrute leant back in his chair, and puffed his cigar calmly while he mused.

What strange things women were! Any man could manage them, if he only reckoned with their temperaments when dealing with them, and paid no heed to their actual words.

Then he turned to the *Morning Post,* which was on a low stand near, and he read again a paragraph which had pleased him at breakfast:

"The Duke of Glastonbury and Lady Ethelrida Montfitchet entertained at dinner last night a small party at Glastonbury House, among the guests being," and here he skipped some high-sounding titles, and let his eyes feast upon his own name, "Mr Francis Markrute."

Then he smiled and gazed into the fire, and no one would have recognised his hard blue eyes, as he said softly:

"Ethelrida, *belle et blonde.*"

* * *

While the financier was contentedly musing in his chair beside the fire, his niece was hurrying into the park, wrapped in a dark cloak and thick veil.

Zara Shulski shivered in spite of the big cloak, as she peered into the gloom of the trees.

The rendezvous had been for six o'clock, and it was now twenty minutes past, and it was so bad for Mirko to wait in the cold. Perhaps they would have gone on. But no, she caught sight of two shabby figures.

They came forward eagerly to meet her. In the half-light it could be seen that the boy was an undersized little cripple, of perhaps nine or ten years old, but looking much younger. It could also be seen that, even in his worn overcoat and old stained felt hat, the man was a gloriously handsome creature.

"What joy to see you, Cherisette!" exclaimed the child. "Papa and I have been longing and longing all the day. It seemed that six would never come. But now that you are here let me hug you."

The thin little arms, too long for the wizened body, were clasped fondly round her neck as she lifted him and carried him towards a seat, where the three sat down to discuss their affairs.

"I know nothing, you see, Mimo," the Countess Shulski said, "beyond the fact that you arrived yesterday. I think it was foolish of you to risk it. At least in Paris Madame Dubois would have let you stay, and owe one week's rent, but here, among these strangers . . ."

"Now do not scold us," the man answered, with a charming smile. "Mirko and I felt that the sun had fled when you went last Thursday."

"You are not angry with us, darling Cherisette?" the boy said in a trembling voice.

"My little one! I could never be angry with my Mirko, no matter what he did!"

The two pools of ink softened from the expression of the black panther into the divine tenderness of the Sistine Madonna, as she pressed the frail little body to her side, and pulled her cloak round him.

"Only, I fear it is no use for you to be here in London," she went on. "If my uncle should know it, all hope of getting anything from him might be lost.

"He expressly said, if I would come quite alone, to stay with him for these few weeks, it would be to my advantage, and my advantage means yours; otherwise, do you think I would have eaten of his hateful bread!"

"You are so good to us, Cherisette," the man, Mimo, said. "You have indeed a sister of the angels, Mirko *mio*, but soon we shall all be rich and famous. I had a dream last night, and already

15

I have begun a new picture, of these strange fogs in Grey."

Count Mimo Sykypri was a confirmed optimist.

When the beautiful wife of Maurice Grey, the misanthropic and eccentric Englishman, who lived in a castle near Prague, ran off with Count Mimo Sykypri, her daughter, then aged thirteen, had run with her, and the pair had been wiped off the list of the family.

Maurice Grey, after cursing them both, and making a will depriving them of everything, shut himself up in his castle, and steadily drank himself to death in less than a year. And the brother of the beautiful Mrs Grey, Francis Markrute, never forgave her either.

He refused to receive her or hear news of her, even after poor little Mirko was born, and she married Count Sykypri.

On the father's side the Markrute brother and sisters were of the highest lineage, and even with his bar sinister, the financier could not brook the disgrace of Elinka, he had loved her so! It seemed that her disgrace had frozen all the tenderness in his nature.

Countess Shulski was silent for a few moments, while both Mimo and Mirko watched her face anxiously, she had thrown back her veil.

Then Mirko pressed his arm round his sister's neck, and kissed her cheek, while he cooed love words in a soft Slavonic language, and two big tears gathered in Zara Shulski's deep eyes, and made them tender as a dove's.

She drew out her purse and counted two sovereigns and some shillings from it, which she slipped into Mirko's small hand.

"Keep these, for an emergency," she said. "They are all I have, but I will, I must, find some other way for you soon, and now I shall have to go. If my uncle should suspect that I am seeing you, I might be powerless to help further."

They walked with her to the Grosvenor Gate, and reluctantly let her leave them.

On arriving home, she went straight up to her room, and her eyes filled with tears as she thought of her mother. She had died in cold and poverty in a poor little studio in Paris, in spite of her daughter's and Mimo's frantic letters to Uncle Francis for help.

And now came the memory of her solemn promise. Mirko should never be deserted, her adored mother could die in peace about that, and her last words came back now.

"I have been happy with Mimo, after all, my Cherisette, you and Mimo and Mirko. It was worthwhile . . ." and so she had gasped and died.

Zara knew what she had to do. There was no other way. To her uncle's bargain she must consent, and without further hesitation she went down the stairs.

Francis Markrute was still seated in his library.

He rose from his chair, as she entered the room, with a quiet smile. So she had come! He had not relied upon his knowledge of a woman's temperament in vain.

She was very pale. The extra whiteness showed even on her gardenia skin, and her great eyes gleamed sullenly from beneath her lowering brows of ink.

"If the terms are for the certain happiness of Mirko ... I consent," she said.

Chapter
Two

The four men, the two railway magnates, Francis Markrute, and Lord Tancred, had all been waiting a quarter of an hour before the drawing-room fire when the Countess Shulski sailed into the room.

She wore an evening gown of thin, black, transparent woollen material, which clung round her with the peculiar grace which even her poorest clothes acquired.

Francis Markrute was too annoyed at the delay of her coming to admire anything, but even he, as he presented his guests to her, could not help remarking that he had never seen her look more wonderful, or more contemptuously regal.

They had had a stormy scene in the library half an hour before. Her words had been few, but their displeasure had been unconcealed. She would agree to the bare bargain, if so be this strange man were willing, but she demanded to know the reason of his willingness.

When she was told it was a business matter between the two men and that she would be given a large fortune, she expressed no more surprise than a disdainful curl of the lips.

For her, all men were either brutes, or fools, like poor Mimo.

If she had known that Lord Tancred had already refused her hand, and that her uncle was merely counting upon his unerring knowledge of human nature, and Lord Tancred's nature in particular, she might have felt humiliation, instead of impotent rage.

The young man for his part had arrived exactly on the stroke of eight, a rare effort of punctuality for him. Some underneath excitement to see his friend Markrute's niece had tingled in his veins from the moment he had left the house.

What sort of a woman could it be who would be willing to marry a perfect stranger for the sake of his title and position? And the quarter of an hour's wait had not added to his calm.

So when the door eventually opened for her entry, he had glanced up with intense interest, and had then drawn in his breath, as she advanced up the room. The physical part of the lady was at all events extremely attractive.

But when he was presented, and his eyes met hers, he was startled by the look of smouldering, sombre hate he saw in them.

What could it all mean? Francis must have been romancing. Why should she look at him like that if she were willing to marry him? He was piqued and interested.

She spoke not a word as they went down to dinner, but he was no raw youth to be snubbed into silence; his easy polished manner soon started a conversation upon the usual everyday things.

He received "Yes" and "No" for answers, and the railway magnate on her other side was hardly more fortunate.

The part which particularly irritated Lord Tancred was that he felt sure she was not really stupid, who could be stupid with such a face! And he was quite unaccustomed to being ignored by women. Such an experience had not occurred in the whole of his life.

He watched her narrowly. He had never seen so white a skin, and the admirably formed bones of her short small face were covered with an exquisite velvety skin.

She filled him with the desire to touch her, to clasp her tightly in his arms, to pull down that glorious hair and bury his face in it.

When the grouse was being handed he did get a whole sentence from her, in answer to his question of whether she liked England.

"How can one say, when one does not know?" she said. "I have only been here once before, when I was quite a child. It seems cold and dark."

"We must persuade you to like it better," he answered, trying to look into her eyes, which she had instantly averted, the expression of resentment still smouldered there, he had noticed, during their brief glance.

An unusual excitement was permeating his being, he could not account for how or why; he had felt no sensation like it before.

Francis Markrute had been watching things minutely, while he kept up his suave small-talk with Colonel Macnamara on his right hand.

He was well pleased with the turn of events. After all, nothing could have been better than Zara's being late. Now if she only kept up this attitude of indifference, which she seemed likely to do, things might be settled this very night.

Lord Tancred could not get her to have a single continued conversation for the remainder of dinner; and he was raging with annoyance.

When at the first possible moment after the dessert arrived she swept from the room, her eyes met his, as he held the door, and they were again full of contemptuous hate.

He returned to his seat with his heart actually thumping in his side!

All through the laborious conversation upon Canada, and how best to invest a capital, which Francis Markrute, with great skill and apparently hearty friendship, prolonged to its utmost limits, he felt the attraction and irritation of this strange woman grow and grow.

He no longer took the slightest interest in the pros and cons of his future in the colony! And when at last he heard the distant tones of Tschaikovsky's "Chanson Triste," as they ascended the stairs, he came suddenly to a decision.

She was sitting at the grand piano in the back part of the room. A huge, softly shaded lamp shed its veiled light upon her white face and rounded throat.

Her hands and arms, which showed to the elbow, seemed not less pale than the ivory keys, and those pools of dark mystery had a whole world of anguish in their depths.

For this was the tune that her mother had loved, and she was playing it to remind herself of her promise, and to keep herself firm in her determination to accept the bargain for her little brother Mirko's sake.

She glanced at Lord Tancred as he entered, and thought that he was a splendid physical creature, who would be strong, and horrible probably, like the rest!

The whole expression of her face changed as he came and leaned upon the piano. The sorrow died out of her eyes, and was replaced by a fierce defiance, and her fingers broke into a tarantella of wild sounds.

"You strange woman!" Lord Tancred said.

"Am I strange?" she answered through her teeth. "It is said by those who know that we are all mad at some time, and at some point. I have, I think, reason to be mad, tonight!"

With that she crashed a final chord, and rose from her seat, and crossed the room.

"I hope, Uncle Francis, your guests will excuse me," she said, with an imperial, aloof politeness, "but I am very tired. I will wish you all a good-night."

She bowed to them as they expressed their regrets, and then slowly left the room.

"Good-night, Madame," Lord Tancred said at the door. "Someday you and I will cross swords."

But he was rewarded by no word, only an annihilating glance from her sullen eyes, and he stood there and gazed at her as she passed up the stairs.

"An extraordinary and beautiful woman, your niece, my dear Markrute," he heard one of the gentlemen say, as he returned to the group by the fire, and it angered him, he could not have told why.

Francis Markrute, who knew his moments, began now to talk about her casually, how she was an interesting, mysterious character. Beautiful, well, no, not exactly that, a superlative skin, and fine eyes and hair, but no special features.

"I will not admit that she is beautiful, my friend," he said; "beauty suggests gentleness and tenderness. My niece reminds me of the black panther in the Zoo, but one could not say if she were tamed."

Such remarks were not calculated to allay the growing interest and frantic attraction Lord Tancred was feeling. Francis Markrute knew his audience, he never wasted his words.

Then he abruptly turned the conversation back to Canada again, until even the two magnates, on their own ground, were bored, and said good-night, and the four men came down the stairs together.

As the others were being helped into their coats he said:

"Will you have a cigar with me, Tancred, before you go on to your supper?"

Presently they were both seated in mammoth armchairs in the cosy library.

"I hope, my dear boy, you have all the information you want about Canada," he said. "You could not find two more influential people than Sir Philip and the Colonel. I asked . . ."

But Lord Tancred interrupted him.

"I don't care a farthing more about Canada!" he flashed out. "I have made up my mind, if you really meant what you said today, I will marry your niece, and I don't care whether she has a cent or not!"

Francis Markrute's plans had indeed culminated with a rush!

But he expressed no surprise, merely raised his eyebrows mildly, as he answered:

"I always mean what I say. Only I do not care for people to do things blindly. Now that you have seen my niece, are you sure she would suit you? It would be no easy task for any man to control her, as a wife."

"I don't care for tame women," Lord Tancred

said. "It is that very quality of difficulty which has inspired me. By George! did you ever see such a haughty bearing! It will take a man's whole intelligence to know which bit to use."

"She may close her teeth on whatever bit you use, and bolt with it. Do not say afterwards that I let you take her blindly."

He paused a moment before he continued:

"I expect you would like to know about her background. She is the daughter of Maurice Grey, a brother of old Colonel Grey of Hintingdon, whom everybody knew. She has been the widow of an unspeakable brute for over a year, and was an immaculate wife, and devoted daughter before that. The possibilities of her temperament are all to come."

Lord Tancred sprang from his chair; the very thought of her, and her temperament, made him thrill. Was it possible that he was already in love, after one evening?

"Now we must really discuss affairs, my dear boy," the financier went on. "Her dower, as I told you, will be princely."

"That I absolutely refuse to do, Francis," Lord Tancred answered. "You can settle the other things with my lawyer if you care to, and tie it all up on her. I am not interested in that matter. The only thing I really wish to know is, are you sure she will marry me?"

"I am perfectly sure," said the financier with narrowed eyes. "I would not have suggested the affair today if I had had any doubts about that."

"Then it is settled, and I shall not ask why. I shall not ask anything, only when may I see her again, and how soon can we be married?"

"Come and lunch with me in the City tomorrow, and we will talk over everything. I shall have seen her, and can tell you then when to present yourself. I suppose you can have the ceremony at the beginning of November?"

"Six whole weeks hence!" Lord Tancred said protestingly. "Must she get such heaps of clothes? Can't it be sooner? I wanted to be here for my Uncle Glastonbury's first shoot on the second of November, and if we are only married then, we shall be off on a honeymoon!"

He paused.

"You must come to that shoot, old boy, by the way, one day's partridge driving and the rest covert shooting, but he only asks the nicest people, and none of the bores to this party, which is also for Ethelrida's birthday."

"It would give me great pleasure to be there," Francis Markrute said, and he looked down, so that Lord Tancred should not see the joy in his eyes.

* * *

When Lord Tancred left the house in Park Lane, he did not go on to the supper at the Savoy as he had promised. Instead he drove straight back to his rooms in St. James's Street.

He had acted upon a mad impulse—he knew

that, and did not argue with himself about it, or regret it. Some force, stronger than anything he had hitherto known, had compelled him to come to the decision.

And what would his future life be like with this strange woman? That could not be guessed, but he did not doubt that it would contain scenes of the greatest excitement.

She would, in all cases, look the part—his mother, daughter of the late and sister of the present Duke of Glastonbury, could not move with more dignity. Which reminded him he had better write to his mother and inform her of his intended marriage.

He paused a moment before he wrote.

My Dear Mother,
I am going to be married at last. The lady is a daughter of Maurice Grey (a brother of old Colonel Grey of Hintingdon, who died last year), and the widow of a Pole named Shulski, Countess Shulski she is called.
[He had paused here, because he suddenly remembered he did not know her Christian name!]
She is also the niece of Francis Markrute, to whom you have such an objection, or had, last season. She is most beautiful, and I hope you will like her. Please call on her tomorrow. I will come and breakfast with you about ten.
Your affectionate son,
Tancred

When his mother read this she leaned back on her pillows and closed her eyes. She adored her son, but she was above all things a woman of the world, and given to making reasonable judgments.

Tristram was past the age of a foolish entanglement, there must be some strong motive in this action. He could hardly be in love. She knew when he was in love! And he had shown no signs of it lately, not really for several years, for a well-conducted affaire with Laura Highford could not be called being in love.

Then she thought of Francis Markrute. He was so immensely rich, and she could not help a relieved sigh. There would be money at all events. But she knew that could not be the reason. She was aware of her son's views about rich wives.

She was aware, too, that with all his sporting tastes, and modern irreverence of tradition, underneath he was of a reserved nature, intensely proud of the honour of his ancient name. What, then, could be the reason for this engagement?

She rang the bell for her maid, and told her to ask the young ladies to put on dressing-gowns and come to her.

Lord Tancred's two sisters were nice, fresh English girls, and stood a good deal in awe of their mother. They kissed her and sat down on the bed.

They felt it was a momentous occasion, because Lady Tancred never saw anyone until her hair was arranged, not even her own daughters!

"Your brother Tristram is going to be married," she said, and she referred to the letter lying on the coverlet, "to a Countess Shulski, a niece of Mr Markrute."

"Oh, Mother!" and "Really!" gasped Emily and Mary.

"Have we seen her? Do we know her?"

"No, I think we can none of us have seen her. She certainly was not with Mr Markrute at Cowes. I suppose Tristram must have met her abroad, he went to Paris, you remember, at Easter, and again in July."

"I wonder what she is like," Emily said.

"Is she young?" Mary inquired.

"Tristram does not say," Lady Tancred replied, "only that she is beautiful."

"How surprising!" both girls gasped together.

"Yes, it is certainly unexpected," their mother agreed, "but Tristram has judgment, he is not likely to have chosen anyone of whom I should disapprove.

"You must be ready to call on her directly after luncheon. Tristram is coming to breakfast, so have yours in your room. I must talk to him."

The girls, who were dying to ask a hundred thousand questions, knew they were dismissed. Kissing their mother, they retired to their own large back room, which they shared in common with all their pleasures and little griefs.

Lady Tancred awaited her son in the small front morning-room. She was quite as much a

30

specimen of an English aristocrat as he was, with her brushed-back grey hair, and beautiful, fine-featured face. Supremely dignified, she dressed well and with perfect taste.

It was nearly eleven o'clock before Tristram made his appearance.

He apologised charmingly. His horse, Satan, had been unusually fresh, and he had been obliged to give him an extra canter twice round the Row. "Is breakfast ready?" he asked, as he was extremely hungry!

Yes, breakfast was ready, and they went into the dining-room.

"Tristram, dear boy, now tell me all about it," Lady Tancred said, when they were alone.

"There is hardly anything to tell you, Mother, except that I am going to be married about the twenty-fifth of October. You will be awfully nice to Zara, won't you?"

He had taken the precaution to send round a note early in the morning to Francis Markrute, asking for his lady's full name, so the "Zara" came out quite naturally!

"She is rather an unusual person," he went on, "and . . . er . . . has very stiff manners. You may not like her at first."

"No, dear?" said Lady Tancred hesitatingly. "Stiff manners, you say? That, at least, is on the right side. I always deplore the modern free-and-easiness."

"There is nothing free and easy about her!"

said Tristram, helping himself to a cutlet, while he smiled grimly.

His sense of humour was highly aroused over the whole thing, only that overmastering "something" which drew him was even stronger than anything else.

Then he felt there was no use in allowing his mother to drag information from him, he had better tell her what he meant her to know.

"You see, Mother, the whole thing has been arranged rather suddenly, and I have told you at once. Zara will be awfully rich, and we shall live at Wrayth, but I need not tell you I am not marrying her for that reason."

"No, I know you," Lady Tancred said, "but I cannot disguise the fact that I am glad she is rich. We live in an age when the oldest and most honoured name is useless without money to keep up its traditions, and any woman would find your title, and your position, well worth all her gold."

She smiled as she went on:

"There are things which you will give her in return, which only hundreds of years can produce. You must have no feelings that you are accepting anything from her which you cannot return in other ways."

"Zara is well bred, she will not throw her money in my teeth," Lord Tancred smiled.

"I will take the girls and call on her immediately after luncheon," Lady Tancred said.

"She may not be in, and in any case, perhaps

for today, only leave cards. Tomorrow or next day I'll go with you."

He paused.

"You see, until the announcement comes out in the *Morning Post*, nothing is quite settled, and I expect Zara would like it better if you did not call until then."

That was probably true, he reflected, since he had not even exchanged personal pledges with her.

As his mother looked stiffly repulsed, his sense of humour got the better of him. He burst into a peal of laughter, jumped up, and kissed her with the delightful caressing boyishness which made her love him more than any of her other children.

"Darling," she murmured, "if you are so happy as to laugh like that, I am happy too, and will do just what you wish."

Her proud eyes filled with tears, as she pressed his hand.

"Mum, you are a dear!" Lord Tancred exclaimed, and kissed her again.

Holding her arm, they went back into the morning-room.

"Please don't say a word to anyone until it is in the *Morning Post* tomorrow morning," he begged as he was leaving.

"Not even to Cyril?" his mother asked. "You have forgotten he is coming up for the day from Eton, and the girls already know."

"Cyril! By Jove! I had forgotten!" Lord Tancred exclaimed. "Yes, tell him, he is a first-class chap, he'll understand, and give him these from me."

He pulled some sovereigns from his pocket, then, with a smile he left.

* * *

Countess Shulski was sitting finishing her breakfast, in the little upstairs sitting-room which Francis Markrute had allotted to her for her personal use, when he tapped at the door, and asked if he might come in.

"I have come to settle the details of your marriage," he said. "You saw Lord Tancred last night. You can have no objection to him on the ground of his person, and he is a very great gentleman, as you will find."

She said nothing.

"I have arranged with him for you to be married in October, about the twenty-fifth. So now comes the question of your trousseau. You must have clothes, to fit you for so great a position. You had better get them in Paris."

He paused, thinking of her splendid carriage, and air of breeding, and it gave him a thrill of pride in her, after all, she was his own niece!

"It will be a very great joy to dress you splendidly," he said. "I would have done so always, if I had not known where the money would go, but we are going to settle all that now, and everyone can be happy."

It was not in her nature to beg, and try to

secure favours for her brother and Mimo, without paying for them.

She had agreed upon the price of herself. Now all she had to do was to obtain for that as much for them as possible.

"Mirko's cough has come back again," she said quietly. "Since I have consented, I want him to be able to go into the warmth without delay. They are here in London now, he and his father, and in a very poor place."

"I have thought it all out," Francis Markrute answered. "There is a wonderfully clever doctor at Bournemouth, where the air is perfect for people who have delicate lungs.

"I have communicated with him, and he will take the child into his own house, where he will be beautifully cared for, and can have a tutor, and gradually, when he is stronger, he can return to Paris or Vienna, and have his talent for the violin cultivated.

"I want you to understand," he continued, "that if you agree to my terms, your brother will not be stinted in any way."

"Are there children in the house?" she asked.

Mirko was peculiar and did not like other little boys.

"The doctor has a little girl, about your brother's age. And she is delicate too, so they could play together."

"I would wish to go down and see the doctor first, and the home," she said.

"You shall do so, of course, when you like, and I will set aside a certain sum every year to be invested for him, so that when he grows up he will have a competence, even a small fortune. I will have a deed drawn out for you to sign."

"That is well," she said. "And now give me some money, please, that I may relieve their present necessities, until my brother can go to this place. I do not consent to give myself, unless I am certain I free those I love from anxieties. I should like immediately a thousand francs, forty pounds of your money, isn't it?"

"I will send the notes up in a few minutes," Francis Markrute replied. "Meanwhile, that part of the arrangement being settled, I must ask you to pay some attention to the thought of seeing your *fiancé*."

"I do not wish to see him," she announced.

"Possibly not, but it is part of the bargain," her uncle smiled. "You can't marry the man without seeing him! He will come and call upon you this afternoon, and no doubt will bring you a ring.

"I trust to your honour not to show your dislike so plainly that no man could carry through his side. Please remember that your brother's welfare depends upon your actual marriage. If you cause Lord Tancred to break off the match, the bargain between you and me is void."

The dark wild creature's look appeared in her eyes, and an icy stillness settled upon her. But she began to speak rather fast, with a catch in the breath between the sentences.

"Since you wish this so much for your own ends, arrange for me to go to Paris, alone, away from him, until the wedding day. He must hate the thought as much as I do.

"Explain to the man that I *will not* go through the degradation of the pretence of an engagement. I will play my part, for the visits of ceremony to his family, but beyond that, after today, I *will not* see him alone, or have any communication with him. Is it understood?"

Francis Markrute looked at her with growing admiration. She was gorgeously attractive in this mood.

"It shall be understood," he said.

He knew it was wiser to insist upon no more, and he knew he could count upon her honour and her pride to fulfil her part of the bargain, if she were not exasperated beyond bearing.

"I will explain everything to Lord Tancred, at lunch," he said, "I will not detain you longer now. You are a beautiful woman, Zara. And I know in time you will be very happy."

"Happy," she answered. "Who is ever happy?"

"In two or three years you will admit to me that you know of four human beings who are ideally happy."

When Zara was alone she clenched her hands, and walked up and down for a few moments, and her whole serpentine body writhed with passionate anger and pain.

Yes, she was a beautiful woman, and had a right to her life and joys, like another, and now she was to be tied and bound again, to a husband!

However, she must tell the others the good part of her news at least, and she rushed out to find a taxi.

But when she arrived she found they were out. She waited and was growing impatient, when at last they came back.

"Cherisette, angel! But what joy!" said Mirko as he hurled himself into her arms.

"I have brought you good news," she said, and she drew out two ten-pound notes. "I have made my uncle see reason. Here is something for the present, and he has such a kind and happy scheme for Mirko's health. Listen, and I will tell you about it."

They clustered round her, while she explained, in the most attractive manner she could, the picture of the boy's future, but, in spite of all that, his beautiful little face fell, as he grasped that he was to leave his father.

"It will only be for a time, darling," Zara said; "just until you get quite well and strong, and learn some lessons. All little boys go to school, and come home for the holidays. You know *Maman* would have wished you to be educated like a gentleman."

"But I hate other boys, and you have taught me so well!"

"Oh! but, Mirko *mio!* it is a splendid idea. Think, dear child, a comfortable home and no anxieties," Mimo said. "Truly your sister is an angel. Your cough will get quite well, and perhaps I can come and lodge in the town, and we could walk together."

But Mirko pouted, and Zara sighed and clasped her hands.

"If you only knew how hard it has been to obtain this much," she said, with despair in her voice. "Oh, Mirko, if you love me you would accept it! I am going down to the place tomorrow to see it, and judge for myself. Won't you be good and try to please me?"

Then the little boy fell to sobbing and kissing her, nestling in her arms with his curly head against her neck, and finally he agreed.

* * *

Neither Lord Tancred nor Mr Markrute was late at the appointment in the City restaurant where they were to lunch.

They spoke of ordinary things for a moment, and then Lord Tancred's impatience to get at the matter which interested him became too great to wait longer, so he said:

"Well?"

"I saw her this morning, and had a talk," the financier said. "You must not overlook the fact which I have already stated to you, she is a most difficult problem. You will have an interesting time, taming her!"

He smiled faintly as he went on:

"For a man of nerve I cannot imagine a more thrilling task. She is a woman who has been restricted in all her emotions and could lavish it all upon the man she loves."

Lord Tancred thrilled as he answered:

"Yes, but I want to find out all about her for myself. I just want to know when I may see her, and what is the programme."

"The programme is that Zara will receive you this afternoon about tea-time. You must explain to her you realise you are engaged. You need not ask her to marry you, she knows it is already settled. Be as businesslike as you can, and come away."

He paused to add slowly:

"She has made it a condition that she sees you as little as possible until the wedding. If you wish to have the slightest success with her afterwards, be careful now. She is going to Paris immediately for her trousseau. She will return about a week before the wedding, when you can present her to your family."

Tristram smiled grimly. Then the two men's eyes met and they both laughed.

"Jove, Francis!" Lord Tancred exclaimed. "Isn't it a wonderful affair, a real dramatic romance here in the twentieth century. Would not everyone think I was mad if they knew!"

"It is madmen of that sort who are often the sanest," Francis Markrute answered, "the world is full of apparently sane fools. You will reopen Wrayth, of course. I wish my niece to be a Queen of Society, and have her whole life arranged with due state."

Tancred nodded.

"I wish your family to understand that I appreciate the honour of the connection with them," Francis Markrute went on, "and that we consider it a privilege, since we are foreigners, that we should provide the necessary money for your life together."

As Lord Tancred listened, he thought of his mother's similar argument at breakfast.

"I'll tell you what, Francis," Tancred said presently, "I would like my cousin Ethelrida to meet Countess Shulski pretty soon, I don't know why, but I believe the two would get on."

"There is no use suggesting any meetings until my niece comes back from Paris," the financier replied, "she will be in a different mood by then."

"It is a long time," Tancred said, in a disappointed voice.

"Let me arrange to give a dinner at my house, at which perhaps the Duke and Lady Ethelrida would honour me by being present, and of course your mother, sisters, and any other member of your family you may wish to ask. Let us say the night of my niece's return."

He drew a small calendar note-book from his pocket.

"That shall be the eighteenth, a Wednesday,

and we will fix the wedding for Wednesday the twenty-fifth, a week later."

He turned the pages.

"That gets you back from your honeymoon on the first of November and you can stay wih me that night. If your uncle is good enough to include me in the invitation to his shoot, we can all three go down to Montfitchet on the following day, the second."

"Yes, that will be fine," Lord Tancred agreed.

* * *

Countess Shulski was seated in her uncle's drawing-room when Lord Tancred was announced, and she rose as he advanced towards her.

"You understand why I have come," he said.

"Yes."

"I want to marry you."

"Really."

"Yes, I do."

He set his teeth, certainly she was difficult!

"That is fortunate—since you are going to do so."

This was not encouraging, it was also unexpected!

"We are to be married, with your permission, on the twenty-fifth of October."

"I have already consented," Zara answered, and clasped her hands.

"May I sit down beside you and talk?" Tancred asked.

She pointed to a Louis XVI *bergere* which stood opposite, and she took a small armchair at the other side of the fire.

They sat down, she gazing into the blazing coals, and he gazing at her. How could so voluptuous-looking a creature be so icily cold? he wondered. Her wonderful hair seemed burnished like dark copper, in the light of the fire, and that gardenia skin was temptation itself.

He was so thrilled with a mad desire to kiss her, he had never in his life felt so strong an emotion towards a woman.

"Your uncle tells me you are going away to-morrow, and that you will be away until a week before our wedding, but I suppose you go to buy your clothes?"

"Yes, I must."

He got up, he could not sit still, he was too wildly excited. He stood leaning on the mantelpiece quite close to her, his eyes devouring her with the passionate admiration he felt.

She glanced up, and when she saw their expression, her jet brows met, while a look of infinite disgust crept over her face.

He was just like all men, a hateful, sensual beast. She knew he desired to kiss her, to kiss a person he did not know! Her experience of life had not encouraged her to make the least allowance for the instinct of man.

For her, that whole side of human beings was

simply revolting. In the far-back recesses of her mind, she knew and felt that caresses and such things might be good, if one loved, passionately loved, but in the abstract, just because of the attraction of sex, they were hideous.

To her Tristram appeared a satyr, but she was no timid nymph, but a fierce panther, ready to defend herself!

He saw her look, and drew back.

This was going to be much more difficult than he had imagined, and he knew he must keep himself under complete control. So he turned away to the window and glanced out on the wet park.

"My mother called upon you today, I believe," he said at last. "I asked her not to expect you to be at home. It was only to show you that my family will welcome you with affection."

"It is very good of them."

"The announcement of the engagement will be in the *Morning Post* tomorrow. Do you mind?"

"Why should I mind," she said in a surprised voice. "Since it is true, the formalities must take place."

"It seems as if it could not be true. You are so frightfully frigid," he said with faint resentment.

"I cannot help how I am," she said, in a tone of extreme hauteur. "I have consented to marry you, I will go through with all the necessary ceremonies, but I have nothing to say to you. Why should we talk when once those things are settled?

You must accept me as I am or leave me alone, that is all."

Then suddenly her temper made her add, in spite of her uncle's warning:

"For I do not care!"

He turned now, he was angry, and nearly flared up, but the sight of her standing there, magnificently attractive, stopped him. This was merely one of the phases of the game, he should not allow himself to be worsted by such a speech.

"I expect you don't, but I do," he said, "and I am quite willing to take you as you are, or will be."

"Then that is all that need be said," she answered coldly. "Arrange with my uncle when you wish me to see your family, on my return. I will carry out what he settles, and now I need not detain you, and will say good-bye."

"I am sorry you feel you want to go so soon," he said, "but good-bye."

He let her pass out, without shaking hands.

When he was alone in the room he realised he had not given her the engagement ring, which still lay in his pocket!

He looked round for a writing-table, and finding one sat down and wrote her a few words.

I meant to give you this ring. If you don't like sapphires, it can be changed. Please wear it.
And believe me to be
Yours,
Tancred

He put it with the little ring case, and enclosed both on a large envelope, and then he rang the bell.

"Send this up to the Countess Shulski," he said to the footman who presently came, "and is my motor at the door?"

It was, so he descended the stairs.

"To Glastonbury House," he ordered his chauffeur, and then leaned back against the cushions.

Ethelrida might be having tea, and she was always so soothing and sympathetic.

"Yes, Her Ladyship was at home," he was told when he arrived, and he was shown up into his cousin's sitting-room.

Lady Ethelrida Montfitchet had kept house for her father, the Duke of Glastonbury, ever since she was sixteen, when her mother died.

She acted hostess at the ducal parties with the greatest success. She was about twenty-five, and one of the sweetest of young women.

She was very tall, rather plain, and very distinguished, but Francis Markrute thought her beautiful.

She was strikingly fair, with silvery light hair, and kind, wise, grey eyes, and her figure, in its slenderness, was a thing which dressmakers adored; there was so little of it that any frock could be made to look well on it.

"I have come to tell you such a piece of news, Ethelrida," Lord Tancred said. "Guess what it is!"

"How can I, Tristram? Is Mary really going to marry Lord Henry?"

"Not that I know of, yet, but I daresay she will someday. No, guess again, it is about a marriage."

"A man or a woman?" she asked meditatively, as she poured him out some tea.

"A man—me!" he said, with reckless grammar.

"You! Tristram!" Lady Ethelrida exclaimed, with as much excitement as she ever permitted herself. "You are going to be married, but to whom?"

"I am going to be married to a widow, a niece of Francis Markrute's, you know him."

Lady Ethelrida nodded.

"She is the most wonderfully attractive creature you ever saw, Ethelrida. She has stormy black eyes, no, they are not really black, they are slate colour, and red hair, and a white face. And do you know, I believe I am awfully in love with her!"

"You only 'believe,' Tristram, that sounds odd as a reason for marriage!" Lady Ethelrida could not help smiling.

He sipped his tea, and then jumped up.

"She is the kind of woman a man would go perfectly mad about when he knew her well! I shall—I know."

Then, as he saw his cousin's humorous expression, he laughed boyishly.

"It does sound odd, I admit," he said, "the inference is that I don't know her well, and that is just it, Ethelrida! But only to you would I admit it.

"We are going to be married on the twenty-fifth of October, and I want you to be awfully nice to her. I believe she has had a miserably unhappy life."

"Of course I will, Tristram dear," said Lady Ethelrida, "but I am completely in the dark, when did you meet her? Can't you tell me something more? Then I will be as sympathetic as you please."

Lord Tancred sat down on the sofa beside her, and told her the bare facts.

She gathered enough from his rather incoherent recital to make her see that some very deep and unusual current must have touched her cousin's life.

"I want Uncle Glastonbury to ask Francis Markrute to the shoot on the second of November, Ethelrida," he said, "and you will let me bring Zara, she will be my wife by then, although I was asked only as a bachelor."

"It is my party, not Papa's, you know that," Lady Ethelrida replied, "and of course you shall bring your Zara, I will write and ask Mr Markrute. In spite of Aunt Jane, who says that he is a cynical foreigner, I like him!"

Chapter Three

Society was absolutely taken aback when it read in the *Morning Post* the announcement of Lord Tancred's engagement! No one had heard a word about it.

There had been talk of his going to Canada, and much chaff upon that subject, so ridiculous! Tancred emigrating!

But of a prospective bride, the most gossip-loving busybody at the Marlborough or the Travellers' had never heard! It fell like a bombshell.

And Lady Highford, as she read the news, clenched her pointed teeth. So he had drifted beyond her after all! He had often warned her he would, at the finish of one of those scenes she was so fond of creating.

It was true then, when he had told her before Cowes, that everything must be over, and she had thought his silence since had only been sulking! And who was the creature?

"Niece of Francis Markrute, Esquire, of Park Lane."

Here was the reason, Money! How disgusting men were, they would sell their souls for money! But the woman should suffer for this, and Tristram too, if she could manage it!

Then she cried some tears of rage, he was so adorably good-looking, and had been such a feather in her cap, although she had never been really sure of him.

She had a dose of sal volatile, and dressed with extra care to lunch at Glastonbury House, there she might hear all the details, only Ethelrida was so superior, and uninterested in news or gossip.

There was only a party of five assembled, when she arrived, and she could certainly chatter about Tristram, and hear all she could.

"Is not this wonderful news about your nephew, Duke! No one expected it of him just now, though I, as one of his best friends, have been urging him to marry for the last two years. Dear Lady Tancred must be so enchanted."

"I am sure you gave him good counsel," said the Duke.

"And what is the charming lady like? You all know her, of course?" she asked.

"Why, no," said His Grace. "The uncle, Mr Markrute, dined here the other night, but Ethelrida and I have never met the niece. Of course no one has been in town since the Season, and she was not here then."

"This is thrilling!" said Lady Highford. "An unknown bride! Have you not even heard what she is like, young or old? A widow always sounds so attractive!"

"I am told that she is perfectly beautiful," said Lady Ethelrida from the other side of the table, "and Tristram seems so happy, she is quite young, and very rich."

But this was not what Lady Highford had come for. She wanted to hear everything she could about her rival, to lay her plans, and the moment Ethelrida was engaged with the politician, and the Duke had turned to Mrs Radcliffe, she tackled Ethelrida's cousin in a lower voice.

But he, Jimmy Danvers, had only read what she had that morning. He had seen Tristram at the Turf on Tuesday, after lunch, the day before yesterday, and he had only talked of Canada, and not a word of a lady, it was a bolt from the blue.

"And when I telephoned to the old boy this morning," he said, "and asked him to take me to call upon his damsel today, he told me she had gone to Paris, and would not be back until a week before the wedding!"

"How very mysterious!" piped Laura. "Tristram is off to Paris too, then, I suppose?"

"He did not say, he seemed in the deuce of a hurry, and put the receiver down."

"He is probably only doing it for money, poor darling boy!" she said sympathetically. "It was quite necessary for him."

"Oh, that's not Tristram's measure," Sir James Danvers interrupted. "He'd never do anything for money, I thought you knew him awfully well."

"Of course I do!" Laura snapped out, and then laughed. "But you men! Money would tempt any of you!"

"You may bet your last farthing, Lady Highford, Tristram is in love, he'd not have been so silent about it all otherwise."

"They won't be happy long!" she said. "Tristram could not be faithful to anyone."

"I don't think he's ever been in love before," the blundering cousin continued. "He's had lots of little affairs, but they have only been come and go."

Lady Highford crumbled her bread, and then turned to the Duke—there was nothing further to be got out of this quarter.

Finally lunch came to an end, and the three ladies went up to Ethelrida's sitting-room, and Mrs Radcliffe took her leave to catch a train, so the two were left alone.

"I am so looking forward to your party, dear Ethelrida," Lady Highford cooed. "I am going back to Hampshire tomorrow, but the end of the month I come up again and will be with you in Norfolk on the second."

"I was just wondering," said Lady Ethelrida,

"if after all you would not be bored, Laura? It will be rather a family sort of collection and not so amusing this year, I am afraid, Em and Mary, and Tristram and his new bride, and Mr Markrute, and the rest as I told you."

"Why, my dear child, it sounds delightful. I shall long to meet the new Lady Tancred. Tristram and I are such dear friends, poor darling boy. I must write and tell him how delighted I am with the news, do you know where he is at the moment?"

"He is in London, I believe. Then you really will stick to us and not be bored? how sweet of you!"

And when she had gone, Lady Ethelrida sat down and wrote her cousin a note. Just to tell him, in case she did not see him before she went back to the country tomorrow, that her list, which she enclosed, was made up for her November party.

But if he would like anyone else for his bride to meet, he was to say so.

She added that some friends had been to lunch, and among them Laura Highford, who had said the nicest things and wished him every happiness.

Lady Ethelrida was not deceived about these wishes, but she could do no less than repeat them.

The Duke came into her room just as she was finishing, and warmed himself by her wood fire.

"The woman is a cat, Ethelrida," he said, without any preamble.

"I am afraid she is, Papa. I have just been writing to Tristram, to let him know she insists upon coming still to the shoot. She can't do anything there, and they may as well get it over. She will have to be civil to the new Lady Tancred in our house."

"Whew!" whistled the Duke. "You may have an exciting party. You had better go and leave our cards today on the Countess Shulski, and another of mine as well for the uncle. We'll have to swallow the whole lot, I suppose."

"I rather like Mr Markrute, Papa," Ethelrida said. "I talked to him the other night for the first time, he is extremely intelligent. We ought not to be so prejudiced, just because he is a foreigner."

Meanwhile Zara Shulski had arrived at Bournemouth. The doctor appeared to be all that was kind and clever, and his wife gentle and sweet. Mirko could not have a nicer home, it seemed.

Their little girl was away at her grandmother's for the next six weeks, they said, but would be enchanted to have a little boy companion, and everything was arranged satisfactorily.

Zara stayed the night, and next day, having wired to Mimo to meet her at the station, she returned to London.

They talked in the Waterloo waiting-room, and poor Mimo seemed so glad and happy. She was going back to her uncle's, and was to take Mirko down on the morrow, and on the following day start herself for Paris.

"But I can't go back to Park Lane without seeing Mirko now," she said. "I did not tell my uncle what train I was returning by; there is plenty of time. I will go and have tea with you at Neville Street; it will be like old times."

At that moment there passed them in Whitehall a motor-car going very fast, the inmate of which, a handsome young man, caught the most fleeting glimpse of them; hardly enough to be certain he recognised Zara. But it gave him a great start and thrill.

"It cannot be she," he said to himself. "She went to Paris yesterday, but if it is, who is the man?"

* * *

The next three weeks passed for Lord Tancred in continuously growing excitement. He had much business to see to, for the reopening of Wrayth, which had been closed now for the past two years.

He had decided to let Zara choose her own rooms, and decorate them as she pleased, when she should get there. But the big state apartments, with their tapestries and pictures, would remain untouched.

His thoughts were continually with Zara, and what she would be likely to wish. And in the evening when he sat alone in his own sanctum, after a hard day with electricians and workpeople, he would gaze into the blazing logs and dream.

His plan was to go to Paris to the Ritz for the

honeymoon. Zara, who did not know England, would probably hate the solemn servants staring at her in those early days if he took her to Orton, one of the Duke's places, which he had offered to him for the blissful week.

Paris was much better, because he knew it would not all be plain sailing by any means! And every time he thought of that aspect, his keen blue eyes sparkled with the instinct of the chase.

And when they were used to each other, at the end of the week, there would be the party at Montfitchet, where he would have the joy and pride of showing his beautiful wife.

Then, when these gaieties were over, he and Zara would come here to Wrayth! And he could not help picturing how he would make love to her, in this romantic setting.

And perhaps, soon, she would love him too, and then when he got thus far in his picturings, he would shut his eyes, and stretch out his long limbs and call to Jake, his solemn bulldog, and then pat his wrinkled head.

Zara, in Paris, was more tranquil in mind than was her wont. Mirko had not made much difficulty about going to Bournemouth.

Everything was so pretty the day she took him there, the sun shining gaily, and the sea almost as blue as the Mediterranean.

Mrs Morley, the doctor's wife, had been so gentle and sweet, and had taken him to her heart at once, petted him, and talked of his violin.

The parting with poor Mimo had been very moving, they had said good-bye in the Neville Street lodging. Zara thought it was wiser not to risk a scene at the station.

They had kissed and clasped each other. Father and son had both wept, and Mimo had promised to come to see Mirko soon. So at last they had got off.

Then there had been another painful wrench when Zara had left Bournemouth. She had put off her departure until the afternoon of the following day. Mirko had tried to be as brave as he could, but the memory of the pathetic little figure, as she last saw him waving to her from the window, made her tears brim over and splash onto her gloves.

In her short life, with its many moments of deep anguish, she had seldom been able to cry, there were always others to be thought of first.

An iron self-control was one of her inheritances from her grandfather the Emperor, just as her voluptuous, undulating grace, and the red, lustrous hair, came from the beautiful opera dancer and great artiste, her grandmother.

She had cautioned Mrs Morley, if she should hear Mirko often playing the "Chanson Triste," she was to let her know, and she would come to him. It was a sure indication of his state of mind.

She had written to Mimo from Paris, and told him she was going to be married, and that she was doing so because she thought it was best for them all.

He had written back enchanted exclamations of surprise and joy; and had told her she should have his new picture, the London fog, for his wedding gift.

Poor Mimo! so generous always with all he had.

Mirko was not to be told until she was actually married.

She had written to her uncle and asked him, as a great favour, that she might only arrive the very day of the family dinner-party. He could plead excess of trousseau business, or what he liked.

She would come by the nine o'clock morning train, so as to be in ample time for dinner, and it would be so much easier for everyone, if they could get the meeting over, the whole family together, rather than the ordeal of private presentations.

Francis Markrute had agreed, while Lord Tancred had chafed.

"I *shall* meet her at the station, whatever you say, Francis!" he had exclaimed. "I am longing to see her."

As the train drew up at Victoria, Zara caught sight of him, and in spite of her dislike and resentment, she could not help noting that her *fiancé* was a wonderfully good-looking man.

She herself appeared to him as the loveliest

thing he had ever seen in his life, with her exquisite new clothes from Paris and air of distinction. If he had thought her attractive before, he felt ecstatic in his admiration now.

Francis Markrute hurried up the platform, and Tristram frowned, but the financier knew it might not be safe to leave them to a *tête-à-tête* drive to the house!

Zara's temper might not brook it, and he had rushed back from the City, and he hated rushing, to be on the spot to make a third.

"Welcome," he said, before Lord Tancred could speak. "You see, we have both come to greet you."

She thanked them politely, and turned to give an order to her new French maid. Some of the expectant boyish joy died out of Tristram's face, as he walked beside her to the waiting motor.

They said the usual things about the crossing, it had been smooth and pleasant, so fortunate for that time of the year, and she had stayed on deck and enjoyed it, and yes, Paris had been charming, and was always a delightful spot to find oneself in.

Tristram said he was glad she thought that, because, if she would consent, he had arranged to go there for the honeymoon, directly after the wedding.

She inclined her head in acquiescence, but did not speak. The matter appeared one of complete indifference to her.

In spite of his knowledge that this would be

her attitude, and he need not expect anything different, Tristram's heart began to sink down into his boots by the time they reached the house.

When they got into the library, and she began to pour out the tea for them, Tristram thought she looked so astonishingly alluring in her well-fitting blue serge travelling dress, and yet he might not even kiss her white, slender hand! And there was a whole week before the wedding.

And after it, would she keep up this icy barrier between them? If so . . . But he refused to think of it.

He noticed that she wore his engagement ring only on her left hand, and the right one was ringless, nor had she a brooch, or any other jewel anywhere.

He felt glad, he would be able to give her everything. His mother had been so splendid about the family jewels, insisting upon handing them over.

"I think I will go and rest now, until dinner-time," she said, and forced a smile as she moved towards the door.

It was the first time Tristram had ever seen her smile, and it thrilled him.

He had the most frantic longing to take her in his arms and kiss her, and tell her he was madly in love with her, and never wanted her to be out of his sight!

* * *

Lady Tancred had unfortunately one of her very bad headaches, an hour before dinner, and in fact before her son had left the Park Lane house, a telephone message came to say she was dreadfully sorry, it would be impossible for her to come.

It was Emily who spoke to Francis Markrute.

"Mother is so disappointed," she said, "but she really suffers so dreadfully, I am sure Countess Shulski will forgive her, and you too. And she wants to know if Countess Shulski will let Tristram bring her to see her tomorrow morning, without any more ceremony, and stay to lunch?"

Thus it was settled, and this necessitated a change in the table arrangements.

Lady Ethelrida would now sit on the host's right hand, and an aunt on the Tancred side, Lady Coltshurst, on his left, while Zara would be between the Duke and her *fiancé*, as before.

At a quarter before eight, Francis Markrute went up to his niece's sitting-room. She was already dressed in a sapphire-blue velvet masterpiece of simplicity.

The Tancred presents of sapphires and diamonds lay in their open cases, on the table, with the splendid Markrute yards of pearls, which her uncle had given her when she arrived home from Paris.

She was standing looking down at them, the strangest expression of cynical resignation upon her face.

"Your gift is magnificent, Uncle Francis," she said, without thanking him. "Which do you wish me to wear? Yours or his?"

"Lord Tancred's. He has specially asked that you put his on tonight," the financier replied. "You look absolutely beautiful. I knew I could trust your taste, the dress is perfection."

"Then I suppose we shall have to go down," she said quietly.

Before they had finished the soup, the Duke was saying to himself that Zara was the most attractive creature he had ever met in his life.

No wonder Tristram was crazy about her, for Tristram's passionate admiration tonight could not have been mistaken by a child!

Lady Ethelrida, from where she sat, could see Zara's face through a gap in the flowers. The financier had ordered a tall arrangement on purpose; if she by chance should look haughtily indifferent, it was better that her expression should escape the observation of all but her nearest neighbours!

However, Lady Ethelrida just caught the picture of her, through an oblique angle, against a background of French panelling.

And with her quiet, calm judgment of people, she was wondering. What was the cause of that strange look in her eyes? Was it that of a stag at bay? Was it temper? Or resentment? Or only just pain?

And Tristram had said the colour was slate

grey; for her part, she saw nothing but pools of jet-black ink.

"There is some tragic story hidden here," she thought, "and Tristram is too much in love to see it," but she felt rather drawn to her new prospective cousin all the same.

The Duke asked Zara if she knew anything about English politics.

"You will have to keep Tristram up to the mark," he smiled; "he has done very well now and then, but he is a rather lazy fellow."

"Tristram," she thought. "So his name is 'Tristram'!"

She had actually never heard it before, or troubled herself to inquire about it, it seemed incredible! It aroused in her a grim sense of humour, and she looked into the old Duke's face for a second and wondered what he would say if she announced this fact!

And he caught the smile, cynical though it was, and continued:

"I see you have noticed his laziness! Now it will really be your duty to make him a first-rate fighter for our cause; the Radicals will begin to attack our very existence presently, and we must all come up to the scratch."

"I know nothing of your politics," Zara said, "as yet. I do not understand which party is which, but I suppose it is like in other countries, everyone wanting to secure what someone above him has got, without being fitted for the administration of what he desires to snatch."

"That is about it," smiled the Duke.

"It would be reasonable if they were all oppressed here as in France before the great revolution, but are they?"

"Oh dear, no!" interrupted Tristram. "All the laws are made for the lower classes. They have openings to rise to the top of the tree if they wish to. It is wretched landlords like my uncle and myself who are oppressed!"

He smiled delightedly, he was so happy to hear her talk.

"Perhaps later I shall find it interesting," Zara said to the Duke.

"We shall have to instruct you thoroughly between us, eh, Tristram, my boy!" the Duke replied. "Then you must have a salon, like the ladies of the eighteenth century; we want a beautiful young woman to draw us all together."

"Don't you think I have found you a perfect specimen, Uncle!" Tristram exclaimed.

He raised his glass, and kissed the brim while he whispered:

"Darling, my sweet lady, I drink to your health."

But this was too much for Zara! He was overdoing the part. And she turned and flashed upon him a glance of resentment and contempt.

As the dinner went on, Ethelrida felt a grow-

ing sense that they were all on the edge of a volcano. She never meddled in other people's affairs,
but she loved Tristram as a brother, and she felt
a little afraid.

"Your niece looks like an empress, a wonderful Byzantine, Roman Empress!" Lady Ethelrida
said to Francis Markrute.

He glanced at her sideways with his clever
eyes. Had she ever heard anything of Zara's par-
entage? he wondered. Then he smiled at himself
for the thought.

"There are certain reasons why Zara should,"
he said. "I cannot answer for the part of her which
comes from her father, Maurice Grey, a very old
English family, I believe, but on her mother's side,
she could have the passions of an artist, and the
pride of a Caesar."

"May I know something about her?" Ethelrida
said. "I do so want them to be happy. Tristram is
one of the simplest and finest characters I have
ever met. He will love her very much, I fear."

"Why do you say 'you fear'?"

Lady Ethelrida reddened a little, a soft, warm
flush came into her delicate face, and made it look
beautiful: she never spoke of love to men.

"Because a great love is a very powerful and
sometimes a terrible thing, if it is not returned in
like measure. And, oh, forgive me for saying so,
but the Countess Shulski does not look . . . as if
she . . . loves Tristram. . . ."

Francis Markrute did not speak for an instant, and then he turned and gazed straight into her eyes gravely as he said:

"Believe me, I would not allow your cousin to marry my niece, if I were not truly convinced that it will be for the eventual great happiness of them both."

He paused.

"Will you promise me something, Lady Ethelrida? Will you help me not to permit anyone to interfere between them, for some time, no matter how things may appear? Give them the chance of settling everything themselves."

Ethelrida looked back at him with a seriousness equal to his own, as she answered:

"I promise."

Nothing could exceed Zara's dignity when they reached the drawing-room above. They stood in a group by the fire in the larger room at first, and Emily and Mary tried to get a word in, and say something nice, in their frank girlish way.

They admired their future sister-in-law so immensely, and if Zara had not thought they were all acting a part, as she herself was, she would have been touched at their sweetness.

As it was, she inwardly froze more and more, while she answered with politeness, and Lady Ethelrida, watching quietly for a while, grew further puzzled. She felt that it was certainly a mask that this extraordinary and beautiful young woman was wearing.

Presently Ethelrida indicated that she and Zara might sit down upon the nearest French sofa.

"I hope we shall all make you feel you are so welcome, Zara, may I call you Zara? It is such a beautiful name, I think."

The Countess Shulski's strange eyes seemed to become blacker than ever, a startled, suspicious look grew in them. What did this mean?

"I shall be very pleased if you will," she said coldly.

Lady Ethelrida was determined not to be snubbed. She must overcome this barrier if she could, for Tristram's sake.

"England and our customs must seem so strange to you," she went on. "But we are not at all disagreeable people when you know us!"

"It is easy to be agreeable when one is happy," Zara said. "And you all seem very happy here."

"What can make you so unhappy, you beautiful thing? with Tristram to love you, and youth and health and riches!" Ethelrida wondered.

"This appears a sweet and most frank lady, but how can I tell? I know not the English. It is perhaps because she is so well bred that she is enabled to act so nicely," Zara thought.

"You have not yet seen Wrayth, have you?" Ethelrida went on. "I am sure you will be interested in it, it is so old."

"Wr . . . ayth . . . ?" Zara faltered.

She had never heard of it! What was Wrayth?

"Perhaps I do not pronounce it as you are

accustomed to think of it," Ethelrida said kindly.

She was absolutely startled at the other's ignorance.

"Tristram's place, I mean. The Guiscards have owned it ever since the Conqueror gave it to them, after the Battle of Hastings, you know.

"It is one of the rarest cases of a property being so long in one family, even here in England, and the title has only gone in the male line too, as yet. But Tristram and Cyril are the very last. If anything happened to them, it would be the end. Oh! We are all so glad Tristram is going to be married!"

Zara's eyes suddenly blazed now at the unconscious insinuation in this speech.

She understood perfectly the meaning of it! The line of the Tancreds should go on through her! But never, never! That should never be!

If they were counting upon that, they were counting in vain. The marriage was never intended to be anything but an empty ceremony. There must be no mistake about this.

What if Lord Tancred had such ideas too? And she quivered suddenly and caught in her breath with the horror of this thought.

Ethelrida felt a sensation of a sort of petrified astonishment. Tristram's *fiancée* was evidently quite ignorant of the simplest facts about him, or his family, or his house!

Her eyes had blazed at Ethelrida's last speech, with a look of self-defence and defiance! and yet

Tristram was evidently passionately in love with her. How could such things be! It was a great mystery. Ethelrida was bewildered and interested.

Francis Markrute guessed the ladies' lonely moments would be most difficult to pass, so he had curtailed the enjoyment of the port and old brandy and cigars to the shortest possible dimensions, Tristram aiding him. His one desire was to be near his *fiancée*.

She had been cruelly cold and disdainful at dinner, whenever she had spoken to him, but he vowed to himself:

"Before a year is out I will make her love me as I love her, so help me God!"

"Mr Markrute, I am troubled," Lady Ethelrida said, as her host entered. "Your niece is the most interesing personality I have ever met, but underneath something is making her unhappy, I am sure. Please, what does it mean?

"Oh, I know I have promised what I did at dinner, but are you certain it is all right? And can they ever be really at peace together?"

"I give you my word," Frances Markrute replied. "There is someone who is dead, whom I loved, who would come back and curse me now, if I should let them marry, with a doubt in my heart as to their eventual happiness."

And Lady Ethelrida looked full at him and saw that the man's cold face was deeply moved and softened.

"If that is so, then I will speculate no more," she said. "I will trust you."

* * *

Satan was unusually fresh the next morning when Tristram took him for a canter round the park. He was glad of it: he required something on which to work off steam. He was in a mood of restless excitement.

During the three weeks of Zara's absence, he had allowed himself to dream into a state of romantic love for her. He had glossed over in his mind her distant coldness, her frigid adherence to the bare proposition, so that to return to that state of things had come to him as a shock.

But this morning he knew he was a fool to have expected anything else. He was probably a great fool altogether, but he had not changed his mind, and was prepared to pay the price of his folly.

After all, there would be plenty of time afterwards to melt her dislike, so he could afford to wait now. He would not permit himself to suffer again as he had done last night.

Then he came in and had his bath, he made himself into a very perfect-looking lover to present himself to Zara at about half past twelve, to take her to his mother's.

She was, if anything, whiter than usual when she came into the library where he was waiting for her. She had heavy bluish shadows under her eyes, and he saw quite plainly that the night before she must have been weeping bitterly.

A great tenderness came over him. What was this sorrow of hers? Why might he not comfort her? He put out both hands, and then, as she remained stonily unresponsive, he dropped them.

"I am ready," said Zara.

As they drove along, he told her he had been riding in the park that morning and had looked up at the house and wondered which was her window.

He asked her if she liked riding, and she said she had not ridden for ten years; the opportunity had not been in her life, but she used to like it when she was a child.

"I must get you a really well-mannered horse," he said joyously.

Here was a subject she had not snubbed him over!

"And you will let me teach you, when we go down to Wrayth, won't you?"

But before she could answer they had arrived at the house in Queen Street.

Michelham, with a beam on his old face, stood inside the door with his footmen, and Tristram said gaily:

"Michelham, this is to be Her new Ladyship, Countess Shulski."

He turned to Zara.

"Michelham is a very old friend of mine, Zara.

71

We used to do a bit of poaching together when I was a boy and came home from Eton."

Michelham was only a servant, and could not know of her degradation, so Zara allowed herself to smile and looked wonderfully lovely, as the old man said:

"I am sure I wish Your Ladyship every happiness, and His Lordship too; and if I may say so, with such a gentleman Your Ladyship is sure to have it."

Lady Tancred had rigidly refrained from questioning her daughters on their return from the dinner-party. She had not even seen them until the morning, when they had both burst out with descriptions of their future sister-in-law's beauty and strangeness, but their mother had stopped them.

"Do not tell me anything about her, dear children," she had said. "I wish to judge for myself without prejudice."

Zara's heart beat when they got to the door and she felt extremely antagonistic. Francis Markrute had left her in entire ignorance of the English customs, for a reason of his own.

He calculated that if he had informed her that on Tristram's side it was purely a love-match, she, with her strange temperament, and sense of honour, would never have accepted it. He knew she would have turned upon him, and said she could be no party to such a cheat.

He, with his calm, calculating brain, had weighed the pros and cons of the whole matter;

to get her to consent for her brother's sake in the
beginning, under the impression that it was a dry
business arrangement, equally distasteful personally to both parties.

And his plan was to leave her with this impression, keep the pair as much as possible apart,
until the actual wedding and then to leave her
awakening to Tristram.

A woman would be impossibly difficult to
please if, in the end, she failed to respond to such
a lover as Tristram! He counted on what he had
called her moral antennae to make no mistake.

It would not eventually prejudice matters, if
the family did find her a little stiff, so long as she
did not actually show her contempt for the apparent willingness to support the bargain.

So now Zara entered her future mother-in-
law's room with a haughty mien, and no friendly
feelings in her heart.

The two women were mutually surprised
when they looked at each other. Lady Tancred's
first impression was:

"She is a very disturbing type, but how well
bred and how beautiful!"

And Zara thought:

"It is possible that, after all, I may be wrong.
She looks too proud to have stooped to plan this
thing. It may be only Lord Tancred's doing, men
are more horrible than women."

"This is Zara, Mother," Tristram said.

Lady Tancred held out her hands, and then

drew her new daughter, who was to be, nearer, and kissed her.

And over Zara there crept a thrill. She saw that the stately lady was greatly moved and no woman had kissed her since her mother's death. Why if it were all a bargain should she tenderly kiss her?

"I am so glad to welcome you, dear," Lady Tancred said, determining to be very gracious. "I am almost pleased not to have been able to go last night. Now I can have you all to myself."

They sat down on a sofa and Zara asked about her head, and Lady Tancred told her the pain was almost gone, and this broke the ice and started a conversation.

"I want you to tell me of yourself," Lady Tancred said. "Do you think you will like this old England of ours, with its damp and its gloom in the autumn, and its beautiful fresh spring? I want you to, and to love your future home."

"Everything is very strange to me, but I will try," Zara answered.

"Tristram has been making great arrangements to please you at Wrayth," Lady Tancred went on. "But of course he has told you all about it."

"I have had to be away all the time," Zara said.

"They are all to be surprises, Mother," Tristram interrupted. "Everything is to be new to Zara

74

from beginning to end. You must not tell her anything of it."

Then Lady Tancred spoke of gardens. She hoped Zara liked gardens; she herself was a great gardener, and had taken much pride in her herbaceous borders and her roses at Wrayth.

And when they got to this stage of the conversation Tristram felt he could safely leave them to each other, so, saying that he wanted to talk to his sisters, he went out of the room.

"It will be such happiness to think of your living again in the old home," the proud lady said. "It was a great grief to us all when we had to shut it up, two years ago; but you will indeed adorn it for its reopening."

Zara did not know what to reply. She vaguely understood that one might love a home, though she had never had one, but the gloomy castle near Prague, and that made her sigh when she thought of it.

But a garden she knew she should love! And Mirko was so fond of flowers. Oh! if they would let her have a beautiful country home in peace, and Mirko to come sometimes and play there, and chase butterflies, with his excited poor little face, she would indeed be grateful to them.

Her thoughts had wandered when she heard Lady Tancred's voice saying:

"I wanted to give you this myself."

She drew a small case from a table near and

opened it, and there lay a very beautiful diamond ring.

"It is my own little personal present to you, my new dear daughter. Will you wear it some-times, Zara, in remembrance of this day and in remembrance that I give into your hands the hap-piness of my son, who is dearer to me than anyone on earth?"

The two proud pairs of eyes met, and Zara could not answer, and there was a strange silence between them for a second.

Then Tristram came back into the room, which created a diversion, and she was enabled to say some ordinary conventional things about the beauty of the stones, and thanks for the gift.

Only, in her heart, she determined never to wear it. It would burn her hand, she thought, and she could never be a hypocrite.

Lunch was then announced, and they went into the dining-room.

Here she saw Tristram in a new light, with only "Young Billy" and Jimmy Danvers, who had dropped in, and his mother and sisters.

He was gay as a schoolboy, telling Billy, who had not spoken a word to Zara the night before, that now he should sit beside her, and was at liberty to make love to his new cousin!

And Billy, aged nineteen, a perfectly stolid and amiable youth, proceeded to start a laborious conversation, while the rest of the table chaffed about things which were Greek to Zara, but which she was grateful for, as saving her from talking, and so enabling her to pass off the difficulties of the situation.

The moment the meal was over, Tristram took her back to Park Lane. He, too, was thankful that the meeting had passed without an incident, so he hardly spoke, and followed her in silence into the house and into the library.

Now that they were alone, the disguises of the part she had played left Zara, and she resumed her usual icy mien.

"Good-bye," she said coldly. "I am going into the country tomorrow for two or three days. I shall not see you until Monday. Have you anything more that it is necessary to say?"

"You are going into the country!" Tristram exclaimed, aghast. "But I will not . . ."

He paused, for her eyes had flashed ominously.

"I mean," he went on, "must you go? So soon before our wedding?"

She drew herself up and spoke in a scathing voice.

"Why must I repeat again what I said when you gave me your ring? I do not wish to see or speak with you. You will have all you bargained for: can you not leave my company out of the question?"

The Guiscard stern, obstinate spirit was thoroughly roused. Tristram walked up and down the room rapidly for a moment, fuming with hurt rage. Then reason told him to wait. He had no intention of breaking off the match no matter what she should do.

This was Thursday, and there were only five more days to get through, until she would be his wife.

He bent forward and took her hand.

"Very well, you beautiful, unkind thing," he said. "But if you do not want to marry me, you had better say so at once, and I will release you from your promise. Because when the moment comes afterwards for our crossing of swords, there will be no question as to who is to be master!"

Zara dragged her hand from him, and with the black panther's glance in her eyes, she turned to the window and stood looking out.

After a second, she said, in a strangled voice: "I wish the marriage to take place. And now, please go."

And without further words he went.

Chapter
Four

On her way to catch the train for Bournemouth the next day, to see Mirko, Zara met Mimo in the British Museum. He had been down to see his son ten days before.

They had met secretly. Mirko had stolen out, and with the cunning of his little brain fully on the alert, he had dodged Mrs Morley in the garden, and fled to the pine-woods near, with his violin; and there met his father, and had a blissful time.

He was certainly better, Mimo said, a little fatter and his cough was better, and he seemed fairly happy, and quite resigned.

But it had rained before the end of their stolen meeting, and Mimo could see that his clothes were wet, so he had made him run back.

He feared he must have got thoroughly soaked, and he had heard nothing since, but one postcard, which said that Mirko had been in bed, though was now much better and longing, longing to see his Cherisette!

"Oh, Mimo! How could you let him get wet!" Zara exclaimed reproachfully. "It may have made him seriously ill. Oh! the poor angel! And I must stay so short a while, and then this wedding."

She stopped abruptly and her eyes became black. For she knew there was no asking for respite.

There was also no use scolding Mimo; she knew of old no one was sorrier than he for his mistakes, for which those he loved best always had to suffer.

He had been too depressed to work, and the picture of the London fog was not much further advanced, and he feared it would not be ready for her wedding gift.

"Oh, never mind!" said Zara. "I know you will think of me and I shall like that better than any present."

She drove to Waterloo Station alone, a gnawing anxiety in her heart. On the journey to Bournemouth her spirits sank lower and lower, until when she got there it seemed as if the old cab-horse would never reach the doctor's trim house.

"Yes, your little brother has had a very sharp attack," Mrs Morley said as soon as she arrived.

Ten days ago, she explained, he had escaped from the garden and was gone at least two hours. He then returned wet through, and was a little light-headed that night, talking of "Maman and the angels" and "Papa and Cherisette."

However, he had so rapidly recovered that

the doctor had not thought it necessary to let anyone know, and when there was no danger, she, Mrs Morley, guessing how busy Zara must be ordering a trousseau, had refrained from writing.

Here Zara's eyes flashed, and she said sternly:

"The trousseau was not of the slightest consequence in comparison to my brother's health."

Mirko was upstairs in his pretty bed-room with his nurse. He was playing with a puzzle and had not been told that his sister was coming. But some sixth sense seemed to tell him she was there and when her footfall sounded on the lower stairs, she heard an excited voice shouting:

"I tell you I will go, I will go to her, my Cherisette!"

The passionate joy he showed at the sight of her made a tightness round Zara's heart. He did not look ill, only in some unaccountable way he seemed to have grown smaller. There was a pink flush in his cheeks.

He must sit on her lap, and touch all her pretty things. She had put on her uncle's big pearl earrings and one string of big pearls, on purpose to show him. He always loved what was beautiful and refined.

"Thou art like a queen, Cherisette," he told her.

She kissed him and when he was ready for his bed, soothed him to sleep in her arms. It was getting late, and she sang a soft Slavonic cradle song, in a low cooing voice.

The next day they played games together, and did puzzles.

He wished, when it grew dusk, and they were to have their tea, to play his violin to her alone, in the firelight. For more than an hour, he drew forth divine sounds tearing at Zara's heartstrings with the exquisite notes, until her eyes grew wet.

At last he began something that she did not know, and the weird little figure moved as in a dance in the firelight, while as one inspired he played this new air. Then he stopped suddenly, with a crash of joyous chords.

"It is Maman who has taught me that!" he whispered. "When I was ill, she came often and sang it to me, and when they gave me back my violin, I found it at once, and now I am so happy."

He gave a little laugh as he went on:

"The tune speaks of the butterflies in the woods, which are where Maman lives, and there is a little white one which flies beside her, with radiant blue wings. And she has promised me that the music will take me to her, quite soon. Cherisette!"

"No, no," Zara cried. "I cannot spare you, darling. I shall have a beautiful garden of my own next summer, and you must come and stay with me and chase real butterflies with a golden net."

This thought enchanted the child. He must hear all about his sister's garden.

By chance, there was an old number of *Country Life* lying on the table. They looked at the pictures, and, by the strangest coincidence, when they came to the weekly series of those beautiful houses she read at the beginning of the article:

"*Wrayth, the property of Lord Tancred of Wrayth.*"

"See, Mirko," she said in a half voice, "our garden will look exactly like this."

The child examined every picture with intense interest. A statue of Pan and his pipes making the centre of a star in the Italian parterre pleased him most.

"Do you see, Cherisette, he too is not shaped as other people are," he whispered with delight. "Look! And he plays music also. When you walk there, and I am with Maman, you must remember that this is me!"

It was with deep grief and foreboding that Zara left him on Monday morning, in spite of the doctor's assurance that he was indeed on the turn to get quite well.

Whether he would ever grow to be a man was always a doubt, but there was no present anxiety, she could be happy on that score.

But all the way back in the train, she saw the picture of the Italian parterre at Wrayth, with the statue of Pan in the centre of the star, playing his pipes.

* * *

The second wedding day of Zara Shulski dawned with a glorious sun. She had not seen her bridegroom or any of the family since she got back from Bournemouth. She had said to her uncle that she could not bear it.

She signed numbers of legal documents, concerning her marriage settlements, without the slightest interest, and then her uncle handed her one which he said she was to read with care. It set forth the provisions for Mirko's life.

Zara read it over, but the legal terms were difficult for her.

"If it means exactly what we agreed upon, Uncle Francis, I will sign it," she said. "That is, that Mirko shall be cared for, and have plenty of money for life."

"Yes, that is what it means," Francis Markrute replied.

She had gone to her room, and spent the night before her wedding alone. She had steadily read one of her favourite books. She could not allow herself a moment to think.

Then, at last, she opened the window and glanced out on the moon. It was there, above her, over the park, so she turned out the lights and, putting on her furs, sat for a while and gazed above the treetops while she repeated her prayers.

Mimo saw her, as he stood in the shadow on the pavement, at the other side of Park Lane. He had come there in his sentimental way, to give her his blessing, and had been standing looking up for some time.

It seemed to him a good omen for dear Cherisette's happiness, that she should have opened the window and looked out on the night.

It was quite early, only about half past ten, and Tristram, after a banquet with his bachelor friends on the Monday night, had devoted his last evening to his mother, and had dined quietly with her alone.

He felt extremely moved, and excited too, when he left. She had talked to him so tenderly, the proud mother, who so seldom unbent.

She told him how marriage was a beautiful but serious thing, and he must love, and try to understand his wife, and then she spoke of her own great love for him, and her pride in their noble name and descent.

"And I will pray to God that you have strong, beautiful children, Tristram, so that there may be in years to come no lack of the Tancreds of Wrayth."

When he got outside in the street, the moonlight flooded the road, so he sent his motor away, and decided to walk. He wanted breathing space, he wanted to think, and he turned down into Curzon Street, and from there across Great Stanhope Street, and into the park.

And tomorrow night, at this time, the beautiful Zara would be his, and they would be dining alone together at Dover, and surely she would not be so icily cold; surely, surely he could get her to melt.

Further visions came to him and he walked very fast, and presently he found himself opposite his lady's house.

An impulse just to see her window overcame him, and he crossed the road and went out the gate, and there on the pavement saw Mimo, also with face turned, gazing up.

In a flash, he thought he recognised that this was the man he had seen that day in Whitehall, when he was in his motor-car, going very fast.

A mad rage of jealousy and suspicion rushed through him.

It was at this moment that Zara opened her window and, for a second, both men saw her slender, rounded figure standing out sharply against the background of the room.

Then she turned and put out the light.

A murderous passion of rage filled Lord Tancred's heart.

He looked at Mimo, and saw that the man's lips were muttering a prayer, and that he had drawn a little silver crucifix from his coat pocket. He stepped close to him and heard him murmur in his well-pronounced English:

"Mary, Mother of God, pray for her, and bring her happiness!"

And his common sense reassured him somewhat. If this man were a lover, he could not pray so, on this, the night before her wedding to another. It was not in human, male nature, he felt, to do such an unselfish thing as that.

Then Mimo raised his soft felt hat in his rather dramatic way to the window, and walked up the street.

And Tristram, a prey to all sorts of conflicting emotions, went back into the park.

*   *   *

It seemed to Francis Markrute that more than half the nobility of England had assembled in St. George's, Hanover Square, the next day, as, with the beautiful bride on his arm he walked up the church.

She wore a gown of dead white velvet, and her face looked the same shade under the shadow of a wonderful picture hat of black velvet and feathers.

The only jewels that she had on were the magnificent pearls which her uncle had given her. There was no colour about her except in her red burnished hair, and her red curved mouth.

The whole company thrilled as she came up the aisle. She looked like the princess in a fairy-tale, but just come to life.

The organ stopped playing, and now, as in a dream, she knew that she was kneeling beside Tristram, and that the Bishop had joined their hands, and she repeated the vows mechanically in a low, quiet voice.

At last the ceremony was over, and Lord and Lady Tancred walked into the vestry to sign their names. And as Zara slipped her hand from the arm of her newly made husband, he bent down his tall head and kissed her lips.

Fortunately the train of coming relations and friends were some way behind them, and the Bishops were looking elsewhere, or they would have been startled to see the bride shiver, and to have seen the expression of passionate resentment which crept into her face.

But the bridegroom saw it, and it stabbed his heart.

When they got into the smart new motor, after passing through the admiring crowds, Zara shrunk into her corner, and half-closed her eyes. Tristram, intensely moved and strained with the excitement of it all, did not know what to think.

But pride made his bride play her part when they reached her uncle's house.

She stood with her bridegroom, and bowed graciously to the countless congratulatory friends of his, who passed and shook hands.

When, soon after they had entered, Lady Tancred had arrived with Cyril and the girls, she had even smiled sweetly for one moment, when that gallant youth had stood on tiptoe and given her a hearty kiss!

He was very small for his age, and full of superb self-possession.

"I think you are a stunner, Zara," he said. "Two of our fellows, cousins of mine, who were in church with me, congratulated me. And now I hope you're soon going to cut the cake?"

Tristram wondered why her mutinous mouth had quivered and her eyes grown full of mist. She was thinking of her own little brother, far away, who did not even know that there would be any cake.

Eventually they had passed through the shower of rice and slippers, and were at last alone in the motor-car again. Once more she shrank into her corner, and did not speak, and he waited patiently until they should be in the train.

Once there, in the reserved saloon, he came over and sat down beside her, and tenderly took her little grey-gloved hand.

But she drew it away from him and moved further off, before he could even speak.

"Zara!" he said pleadingly.

Then she looked intensely fierce.

"Can you not let me be quiet for a moment?" she hissed. "I am tired out."

He saw that she was trembling, and, though he was very much in love, and maddeningly exasperated with everything, he let her rest, and even settled her cushion for her.

Zara stared out the window, her heart beating in her throat. For she knew this was only a delay, because, as her uncle had once said, the English nobility, as a race, were great gentlemen, and this one in particular, and he would not be likely, because of that, to make a scene in the train.

But they would arrive at the hotel presently, and there was dinner to be got through, alone with him, and then, the afterwards. And as she thought of this, her very lips grew white.

The hideous, hideous hatefulness of men! Visions of moments of her first wedding journey with Ladislaus came back to her. He had not shown her any consideration for five minutes in his life.

Everything in her nature was up in arms. She could not be just; with her belief in his baseness, it seemed to her that here was this man, her husband, whom she had seen but four times in her life, and he was not content with the honest bargain, which he perfectly understood.

Not content with her fortune, and her willingness to adorn his house, but he must perforce allow his revolting senses to be aroused! He must desire to caress her, just because she was a woman, and the law would give him the right to, because she was his wife.

But she would not submit to it! She would find some way out!

She had not even noticed Tristram's charm, it was something which drew all other women to him, but had not yet appealed to her. She saw, on the rare occasions in which she had looked at him, that he was very handsome, but so had been Ladislaus, and so was Mimo, and all men were selfish or brutes.

She was half English herself of course, and that part of her, the calm, common-sense part of the nation, would assert itself presently, but for the time, everything was too strained with her resentment at fate.

Tristram watched her from behind his *Evening Standard*, and was unpleasantly thrilled with the passionate hate and resentment, and all the varying storms of feeling which convulsed her beautiful face.

He was extremely sensitive, in spite of his daring insouciance, and his pride. It would be perfectly impossible even to address her again, while she was in this state.

Finally they arrived at the Lord Warden Hotel.

Here the valet and maid had already arrived, and the sitting-room was full of flowers, and everything ready for dinner, and the night.

"I suppose we dine at eight?" Zara said haughtily, and, hardly waiting for an answer, she went into the room beyond, and shut the door.

At a quarter to the hour of dinner her maid was silently brushing her mistress's long, splendid red hair, while Zara stared into the glass in front of her, with sightless eyes and face set.

She was back in Bournemouth, and listening to "Maman's air." It haunted her and rang in her head; and yet underneath, a wild excitement coursed in her blood.

A knock then came to the door, and when Henriette answered it, Tristram passed her by and stepped into his lady's room.

Zara turned round like a startled fawn, and then her expression changed to one of anger and hauteur.

He was already dressed for dinner, and held a great bunch of gardenias in his hand. He stopped abruptly, when he caught sight of the exquisite picture she made, and he drew in his breath.

He had not known hair could be so long; he had not realised she was so beautiful. And she was his wife!

"Darling!" he gasped, oblivious of even the maid, who had the discretion to retire quickly to the bathroom beyond. "Darling, how beautiful you are! You drive me perfectly mad."

Zara held on to the dressing-table, and almost crouched like a panther ready to spring.

"How dare you come into my room like this! Go!"

It was as if she had struck him. He drew back and flung the flowers down into the grate.

"I only came to tell you dinner was nearly ready," he said haughtily, "and to bring you those. But I will wait for you in the sitting-room, when you are dressed."

He turned round and left by the door through which he had come.

Zara called her maid rather sharply, and had her hair plaited and done, and got quickly into her dress. When she was ready, she went slowly into the sitting-room.

She found Tristram leaning upon the mantel-piece, glaring moodily into the flames. He had been very angry just now, and he thought he was

justified; but he knew he was passionately in love,
as he had never dreamed or imagined he could be,
in the whole of his life.

Should he tell her at once about it and implore
her not to be so cold and hard? But no, that would
be degrading.

After all, he had already shown her a proof
of the most reckless devotion, in asking to marry
her, after having seen her only for one night! And
she, what had her reasons been?

Then his tempestuous thoughts went back to
Mimo, that foreign man whom he had seen under
her window. What if, after all, he was her lover,
and that accounted for the reason she resented his,
Tristram's, desire to caress?

All the proud, obstinate fighting blood of the
Guiscards got up in him. He would not be made a
cat's-paw. If she exasperated him further, he would
forget about being a gentleman, and act as a
savage man, and seize her in his arms, and punish
her for her haughtiness!

So it was his blue eyes, not her dark ones,
which were blazing with resentment this time, and
they sat down to dinner in silence, much to the
waiter's surprise and disgust!

Zara felt almost glad that her husband looked
angry. He would then, of his own accord, leave
her in peace.

At the end of their repast, for different reasons, neither of the two felt calm. Tristram's anger

had died down, likewise his suspicions. And then he grew intoxicated again with her beauty and grace.

She was a terrible temptation to him; she would have been so to any normal man, and they were dining alone together, and she was his very own!

The waiters, with their cough at the door, of warning, brought coffee and liqueurs, and then removed the dinner-table and shut the door.

Zara knew she was now practically alone with her lord for the night.

He walked about the room, he did not drink any coffee, and she stood perfectly still. Then he came back to her, and suddenly clasped her in his arms and passionately kissed her mouth.

"Zara!" he murmured hoarsely. "Good God! do you think I am a stone! I tell you I love you madly. Are you not going to be kind to me, and really be my wife?"

Then he saw a look in her eyes that turned him cold.

"Animal!" she hissed, and hit him across the face.

As he let her fall from him, she drew back, panting and deadly white, while, mad with rage at the blow, he stood with flaming blue eyes, and teeth clenched.

"Animal!" again she hissed, and then her words poured forth in a torrent of hate.

"Is it not enough that you were willing to sell

yourself for my uncle's money, that you were willing to take a woman as a bargain, whom you had never even seen! without letting your revolting passions exhibit themselves like this?

"And you dare to tell me you love me! What do such as you know of love? Love is a true and a pure and a beautiful thing not to be sullied like this. It must come from devotion and knowledge. What sort of a vile passion is it which makes a man feel as you do for me? Only that I am a woman.

"Love! It is not love, it is a question of the senses. Any other would do, provided she were as fair. Remember, My Lord, I am not your mistress! and I will not stand any of this! Leave me, I hate you, animal that you are!"

He stiffened and grew rigid with every word that she said, and when she had finished, he was as deadly pale as she herself.

"Say not one syllable more to me, Zara!" he commanded. "You will have no cause to reprove me for loving you again. And remember this, things shall be as you wish between us. We will each live our lives and play the game. But before I ask you to be my wife again, you can go down upon your knees. Do you hear me? Good-night."

And without a word further, he strode from the room.

* * *

The moon was shining brightly, and a fresh breeze had risen when Tristram left the hotel, and walked rapidly towards the pier. He was mad with rage and indignation at his bride's cruel taunts.

The knowledge of their injustice did not comfort him, and though he knew he was innocent of any desire to have made a bargain, and had taken her simply for her beautiful self, still, the accusation hurt and angered his pride.

How dared she! How dared her uncle have allowed her to think such things!

As he gazed down into the moonlit waves, her last words came back with a fresh lashing sting.

"Leave me, I hate you, animal that you are!"

An animal! And this is how she had looked at his love!

A cold feeling came over him. He was very just, and he questioned himself: Was it true? Had it indeed been only that? Had he indeed been unbalanced and intoxicated merely from the desire of her exquisite beauty? Had there been nothing beyond? Were men really brutes?

He walked up and down very fast. What did it all mean? What did life mean? What was the truth of this thing called Love?

But he knew that for his nature, there could be no love without desire, and no desire without love. And then his conversation with Francis Markrute came back to him, the day they had lunched in the City, when the financier had given his views about women.

Yes, they were right, those views. A woman, to be desirable, must appeal to both the body and brain of a man. If this feeling for Zara were only for the body, then it was true that it was only lust.

But it was *not* true, and he thought of all his dreams of her at Wrayth, of the pictures he had drawn of their future life together, of the tenderness with which he had longed for the night.

Suddenly his anger died down, and was replaced by a passionate grief.

One clear decision he had come to. He would treat her with cold courtesy, and they would play the game. To part now in a dramatic manner, the next day after the wedding, was not in his sense of the fitness of things, was not what was suitable or seemly for the Guiscard name.

When he had left Zara, she had stood quite still. For all the pitifully cruel experiences of her life, she was still very young, young and ignorant of any but the vilest of men.

Thus neither bride nor bridegroom, on this their wedding night, knew peace or rest.

They met the next day for a late breakfast. They were to go to Paris by the two o'clock boat. They were both very quiet and pale.

Zara had gone into the sitting-room first, and was standing looking out on the sea, when her husband came into the room, and she did not turn round, until he said "Good-morning" coldly, and she realised that he was there.

Some strange quiver passed over her at the sound of his voice.

"Breakfast should be ready," he went on

calmly, "I ordered it for twelve o'clock. I told your maid to tell you so. I hope that gave you time to dress."

"Yes, thank you," she said.

He rang the bell and opened the papers, which the waiters had piled on the table, knowing the delight of young bridal pairs to see news of themselves!

Zara glanced at her lord's handsome face, and she saw a cynical, disdainful smile creep over it at something he read.

She guessed it was the account of their wedding, and she too took up another paper and looked at the headings.

There was a flaming description of it all, and as she finished the long paragraphs, she raised her head suddenly and their eyes met. And Tristram allowed himself to laugh—bitterly, it was true, but still to laugh.

They did not seem to have much appetite, or to care what they ate, but the coffee being in front of her, politeness made Zara ask how her husband preferred it to be made.

When he answered, no coffee at all, he wanted tea, she was relieved and let him pour it out himself from the side table.

No pair could have looked more adorably attractive and interesting than Lord and Lady Tancred did, as they went to their private cabin on the boat.

They had the large cabin on the *Queen's* upper deck, and it was noticed that until the London train could be expected to arrive, the bridal pair went outside and sat where they could not be observed, with a view of Dover Castle.

But it could not be seen that they never spoke a word, and each read a book.

When it seemed advisable to avoid the crowd, Tristram glanced up and said:

"I suppose we shall have to stay in that beastly cabin now, or some cad will snapshot us. Will you come along?"

"It is going to be really quite rough," he continued, when the door was shut. "Would you like to lie down?"

"I am never the least ill, but I will try to sleep," Zara answered resignedly.

He settled the pillows, and she lay down, and he covered her up: and as he did so, in spite of his anger with her, and all his hurt pride, he had the most maddeningly strong desire to kiss her, and let her rest in his arms!

He turned away brusquely, sat down at the farthest end, where he opened the window to get in some air, and pulled the curtain over it, then tried to go on with his book.

But every pulse in his body was throbbing, and he could not control at last the overmastering desire to look at her.

She raised herself a little, and began taking the finely worked, small-stoned sapphire pins out of her hat. They had been Cyril's gift.

"Can I help you?" he said.

"It is such soft fur, I thought I need not take it off to lie down," she answered coldly, "but there is something hurting in the back."

He took the thing from her with its lace veil, and the ruffled waves of her glorious hair, as she lay there beneath him, nearly drove him mad with the longing to caress them.

How in God's name would they ever be able to live! He must go outside and fight with himself.

She wondered why his face grew so stern, and when she was settled comfortably again, and the ship had started, he left her alone.

It was fortunately so rough that there were very few people about, and he went far forward and leant on the rail and let the salt air blow into his face.

What if in the end this wild passion for her should conquer him, and he should give in, and have to confess that her cruel words did not hinder him from loving her? It would be too ignominious. He *must* pull himself together and firmly suppress every emotion.

He determined to see her as little as possible, when they got to Paris, and when the ghastly honeymoon week should be over, which he had been contemplating with so much excitement and joy, then they would go back to England, and he would take up politics in earnest, and try to absorb himself in that.

Lying in the cabin, Zara was unconscious of any direct current of thought.

She was quite unconscious that already this handsome young husband of hers had made some impression upon her and that underneath, for all her absorption in her little brother and her own affairs, she was growing conscious of his presence.

Strengthened in his resolve to be true to the Guiscard pride, Tristram came back to her as they reached Calais.

❋ ❋ ❋

When they arrived at the Ritz they were taken to the beautiful Empire Suite on the Vendome side of the first floor.

Everything in the way of arrangement was perfection.

"Tomorrow night we can dine out at a restaurant," Tristram said, "but tonight perhaps you are tired and would rather go to bed?"

"Thank you," said Zara.

She thought she would write her letters to Mirko, and tell him of her new name and address.

"We shall have to stay here for the whole boring week," Tristram announced, when at last coffee was on the table and they were alone. "There are certain obligations to which one's position obliges one to conform."

He did not look at her as he went on:

"You understand I will try to make the time as easy to bear for you as I can. Will you tell me what theatres you have not already seen, and

101

we can go somewhere every night, and in the day-time you have perhaps shopping to do; I know Paris well, so I can amuse myself."

Zara did not feel enthusiastically grateful, but she said "Thank you" in a quiet voice.

Tristram lit a cigar, and walked towards the door.

"Good-night, Milady," he said nonchalantly.

Zara sat still by the table; unconsciously she pulled the petals off an unoffending rose.

It was not until about five o'clock the next day that Tristram came into the sitting-room again.

"Milord had gone to the races in the morning, and had left a note for Milady," the maid had said.

Zara lay back on her pillows, and opened it with a strange thrill, and read:

You won't be troubled with me today. I am going out with some old friends to Longchamps. I have said you want to rest from the journey, as one has to say something.

I have arranged for us to dine at the Café de Paris at 7:30 and go to the Gymnase. Tell Higgins, my valet, if you change the plan.

It was not even signed!

Well, it appeared she had nothing further to fear from him; she could breathe more relieved. And now for her day of quiet rest.

But when she had had her lonely lunch and

her letters to her uncle and Mirko were written, Zara found herself drumming aimlessly on the window-panes and wondering if she would go out.

She had no friends in Paris whom she wanted to see. But it was a fine day, and there is always something to do in Paris, perhaps she would go to the Louvre.

However, she sank down into the big sofa opposite the blazing wood fire, and gradually fell fast asleep. She slept until late in the afternoon, and was, in fact, asleep there when Tristram came in.

He did not see her at first; the lights were not on, and it was almost dark in the streets; the fire, too, had burnt low.

He came forward, and then went back again, and switched on the lamps, and with the blaze Zara sat up, and rubbed her eyes.

One great plait of her hair had become loosened and fell at the side of her head, and she looked like a rosy, sleepy child.

"I did not see you!" Tristram gasped.

Realising her adorable attractions, he turned to the fire and vigorously began making it up.

He felt he could not trust himself for another second, so he rang the bell and ordered some tea to be brought, while he went to his room to leave his overcoat. And when he thought the excuse of the repast would be there, he went back.

Zara felt nothing in particular. Yet she was rather on the defensive, looking out for a possible attack.

She had put up her hair during his absence, and now looked wide awake and quite neat.

"I had a most unlucky day," Tristram said, for something to say. "I could not back a single winner. I think I am bored with racing, on the whole."

"It has always seemed boring to me," she said. "If it were to try the mettle of a horse one had bred, I could understand that, or to ride it oneself, and get the better of an adversary! But just with sharp practices, and for money, it seems so common a thing. I never could take an interest in that."

"Does anything interest you?" he hazarded, and then he felt sorry he had shown enough interest to ask.

"Yes," she said slowly, "but perhaps not many games. My life has always been too ordered by the games of others, to take to them myself . . ."

She stopped abruptly. She could not suppose her life interested him much.

But, on the contrary, he was intensely interested, if she had known.

He felt inclined to tell her so, and that the whole thing of the present situation was ridiculous, and that he wanted to know her innermost thoughts.

He was beginning to examine her critically, and take in every point. Beyond his passionate admiration for her beauty, there was something more to analyse.

Zara was looking absolutely beautiful in her lovely new clothes, and although the *tête-à-tête* dinner was quite early at the Café de Paris, there happened to be a large party of men next to them, and Zara found herself seated in close proximity to a nondescript Count, whom she recognised as one of her late husband's friends.

He was a great big, fierce-looking creature. He looked at her devouringly once or twice, when he thought Tristram did not notice, and then began to murmur immensely *intreprenant* love sentences in his own tongue.

She knew he had recognised her. Tristram wondered why his lady's little nostrils were quivering and her eyes flashing.

She was remembering scenes in the days of Ladislaus, and how he grew wild with jealousy. Once he had dragged her back up the stairs by her hair, and flung her onto the bed.

It was always her fault when men looked at her, he assured her. And the horror of the recollection of it all was still vivid enough.

Then Tristram gradually became greatly worried; without being aware that the man was the cause, he yet felt something was going on. He grew jealous and uneasy, and would have liked to have taken her home.

Because of the things to which she was listening, and because of her fear of a row, Zara never spoke a word but sat there looking defiant and resentful.

Tristram could not understand it, and he eventually became annoyed. What had he said or done to her again?

If Zara had told Tristram what her neighbour was saying, there would at once have been a scene. She knew this, and so she remained in constrained silence, unconscious that her husband was thinking her rude, and that he was growing angry.

She was so strung up with fury at the foreigner that she answered Tristram's few remarks at random, and then while he was paying the bill she abruptly rose to leave. And as she did so, the Count slipped a folded paper into the sleeve of her coat.

Tristram thought he saw something peculiar, but was still in doubt. He followed his wife to the door, and helped her into the waiting automobile.

But as she put up her arm in stepping in, the folded paper fell onto the brightly lighted pavement, and he picked it up.

"Why did you not tell me you knew that fellow who sat next to you?" he said in a low constrained voice.

"Because it would have been a lie," she said haughtily. "I have never seen him but once before in my life."

"Then what business have you to allow him to write notes to you?" Tristram demanded, too overcome with jealousy to control the anger in his tone.

She shrank back in her corner.

"I am not aware the creature wrote me any note," she said. "What do you mean?"

"How can you pretend like this," Tristram exclaimed furiously, "when it fell out of your sleeve! Here it is."

"Take me back to the hotel," she said with a tone of ice. "I refuse to go to the theatre to be insulted. How dare you doubt my word! If there is a note, you had better read it and see what it says."

Lord Tancred picked up the speaking-tube and told the chauffeur to go back to the Ritz. And they both sat silent, palpitating with rage.

When they arrived, he followed her into the lift, and up to the sitting-room. He came in and shut the door. Then he almost shouted.

"You are asking too much of me. I demand an explanation. Tell me yourself about it! Here is your note."

Zara took it, with infinite disdain, and, touching it as though it were some noisome reptile, she opened it and read aloud:

" 'Beautiful Comtess, when can I see you again?'

"The vile wretch!" she said contemptuously. "That is how men insult women! You are all the same!"

"I have not insulted you," he flashed. "It is perfectly natural that I should be angry at such behaviour. If I can find this brute again tonight, he shall know that I will not permit him to write insolent notes to my wife."

She flung the hateful piece of paper in the fire, and turned towards her room.

"I beg you to do nothing further about the matter," she said. "The loathsome man was half drunk. It is quite unnecessary to make a scandal."

Tristram, left alone, paced up and down; he was wild with rage, furious with her, with himself, and with the man! With her because he had told her once, before the wedding, that when they came to cross swords, there would be no doubt as to who would be master!

And here, in the third encounter between their wills, she had each time come off the conqueror!

He was furious with himself that he had not leaned forward at dinner to see the man hand the note, and he was frenziedly furious with the stranger, that he had dared to turn his insolent eyes upon his wife.

He would go back to the Café de Paris, and if the man was there, call him to account, and if not, perhaps he could obtain his name.

But the waiters vowed they knew nothing of the gentleman; the whole party had been perfect strangers, and they had no idea where they had gone.

Tancred spent the third night of his honeymoon hunting round the haunts of Paris, but with no success, and at about six o'clock in the morning came back baffled, still raging but thoroughly worn out.

While he was away, Zara could not sleep and, in spite of her anger, was a prey to haunting fears. What if the two had met and there had been bloodshed!

Several times in the night she got out of her bed to listen at the communicating door; but there was no sound of Tristram, and at about five o'clock, exhausted by her anxiety, she fell into a restless sleep, only to wake again at seven with a lead weight on her heart.

She could not bear it any longer! She must know for certain if he had come in! She slipped on her dressing-gown, and noiselessly stole to the door, and with the greatest caution unlocked it, and turning the handle peeped in.

Yes, there he was, sound asleep! His window was wide open, the curtains were pulled back so that daylight streamed in onto his face.

Zara turned round quickly, to re-enter her room, but in her terror of being discovered, she caught the trimming of her dressing-gown on the handle of the door.

Without her being aware of it, a small bunch of tiny ribbon roses fell onto the floor.

Then she got back into bed, relieved in mind, but terrified at what she had done. It would have been an embarrassing position if he had awakened and found her in his room.

The first thing Tristram saw, when he awoke some hours later, was the little torn bunch of silk roses lying close to Zara's door.

He sprang from bed and picked them up. What could they possibly mean? They were her roses, he remembered the dressing-gown that first evening at Dover when he had gone to her room to give her the gardenias.

For one exquisite moment he thought they were a message, and then he noticed that the ribbon had been wrenched off, and was torn.

No, they were no conscious message, but they did mean that she had been into his room while he slept.

Why had she done this thing? He knew she hated him. What possible reason could she have, then, for coming into his bed-room?

He felt wild with excitement. He would see if, as usual, the door between them was locked. He tried it gently. Yes, it was.

Zara heard him, from her side, and stiffened in her bed. The danger of the ways of men was not over! If she had not remembered, unconsciously, to lock the door when she had returned from her terrifying adventure, he would have come in to her.

So these two thought with different emotions with the locked barrier between them.

A few minutes before twelve, they met in the

sitting-room. Zara was on the defensive; Tristram realised this immediately.

The waiters would be coming in with the breakfast soon. Would there be time to talk to her, or had he better postpone it until they were certain to be alone? He decided upon this latter course, and just said a cold good-morning and opened the New York *Herald* to look at the news.

Zara felt more reassured.

They sat down to their breakfast, each ready to play the game.

Tristram rose, he had finished his coffee. He stood beside her, with an expression upon his face which ought to have melted any woman.

"Zara," he said softly, "I want you to tell me, why did you come into my bed-room?"

Her great eyes filled with startled horror and surprise and her white cheeks grew bright pink with an exquisite flush.

"I?" and she clenched her hands. "I was so . . . frightened . . . that . . ."

Tristram took a step nearer and sat down by her side. He saw the confession was being dragged from her, and he gloried in it, and would not help her out.

She moved further from him, then with grudging reluctance she continued:

"There could have been an unpleasant quarrel. It . . . was so very late . . . I . . . I . . . wished to be sure that you had come back safely."

Then she looked down, and the colour died out of her face, leaving it very white.

"It mattered to you, then, in some way, that I should not come to harm?"

"Yes, of course it mattered," she faltered, and then went on coldly, as he gave a glad start: "Scandals are so unpleasant . . . and scenes are so revolting. I had to endure many of them in my former life."

Oh! So this was it! Just for fear of a scandal, not a jot of feeling for himself! Tristram walked to the fireplace. He was cut to the heart.

The case was utterly hopeless, he felt. He was frozen and stung each time he even allowed himself to be human and hope. But he was a strong man, and this should be the end of it. He would not be tortured again.

He took the little bunch of flowers out of his pocket and handed it to her quietly, while his face was full of pain.

"Here is the proof of your kind interest," he told her. "Perhaps your maid will miss it, and wish to sew it on."

Then, without another word, he went out of the room.

Zara, left alone, sat staring into the fire. What did all this mean? She felt very unhappy, but not angry or alarmed. She did not want to hurt him. Had she been very unkind?

But there were facts which could not be forgotten. He had married her for her uncle's money, and then shown at once that she tempted him.

She got up and walked about the room. She felt uneasy but did not know why.

Did she wish him to come back? Should she go out for a walk? And then, for no reason on earth, she suddenly burst into tears.

* * *

At last Wednesday morning came, and they could go back to England. From that Saturday night, until they left Paris, Tristram's manner of icy polite indifference to Zara never changed.

He avoided every possible moment of her society he could, and when forced to be with her, seemed aloof and bored.

And the freezing manner of Zara was caused no longer by haughty self-defence, but because she was numb at heart.

An unknown, undreamed-of emotion came over her, whenever she chanced to find him close, and during his long absences her thoughts followed him, sometimes with wonderment.

Just as they were going down to start for the train on the Wednesday morning, a telegram was put into her hand. It was addressed "La Baronne de Tancred," and she guessed at once this would be Mimo's idea of her name.

Tristram, who was already down the steps by the concierge's desk, turned and saw her open it, with a look of intense strain. He saw that, as she read, her eyes widened and stared out in front of them for a moment, and that her face grew extra pale.

"Mirko not quite so well," Mimo had written.

She crumpled the blue paper in her hand and followed her husband through the bowing personnel of the hotel, into the automobile. She controlled herself and was even able to give one of her rare smiles in farewell; but when they started she leaned back, and her face was very pale.

Tristram was moved. Who was her telegram from? She did not tell him, and he would not ask, but the feeling that there were things and interests in her life, of which he knew nothing, did not please him.

It had caused her some deep emotion, he could plainly see that. He longed to ask her, but was far too proud. Their relationship had grown so distant, he hardly liked to express even solicitude, which, however, he did.

"I hope you have not had any bad news?"

She turned her eyes upon him, and he saw that she had hardly heard him; they looked blank.

"What?" she asked vaguely, and then, recollecting herself confusedly, went on:

"No, not exactly ... but something about which I must think."

When they got to the station, he suddenly

perceived that she was not following him, but had gone over to the telegraph office.

He waited and fumed. It was evidently something about which she wished no one to see what she wrote, for she could perfectly well have given the telegram to Higgins.

She returned in a few moments, and she saw that Tristram's face was very stern. It did not strike her that he was jealous about the mystery of the telegram; she thought he was annoyed in case they should be late, so she said hurriedly:

"There is plenty of time."

"Naturally," he answered stiffly, as they walked along, "but it is quite unnecessary for Lady Tancred to struggle through this rabble, and take telegrams herself. Higgins could have done it when we were settled in the train."

"I am very sorry," she said, with unexpected meekness.

Tristram did not even make a pretence of reading the papers when the train moved on; he sat there, staring in front of him, with his handsome face shadowed by a moody frown.

Any close observer who knew him would have seen that there was a change in his whole expression since the same time the last week.

The impossible disappointment of everything! What kind of a nature could his wife have, to be so absolutely mute and unresponsive as she had been?

He felt glad he had not given her the chance to snub him again!

How long would it be before he should cease to care for her? He hoped to God it would be soon, because the strain of crushing his passionate desires was one which no man could stand long.

Finally, after the uncomfortable hours, they arrived at Calais and went to the boat.

Here Zara seemed to grow anxious and on the alert. She asked Higgins to enquire if there was a telegram for her, addressed to the ship.

There was not, and she subsided once more, and sat down in their cabin.

Tristram did not even attempt to play the part of the bridegroom. After seeing to her comfort, he left her immediately, and remained on deck for the whole voyage.

When they reached Dover, Zara's expectancy showed again, but it was not until they were just leaving the station that a telegram was thrust through the window. Tristram took it from the boy, and he could not help noticing the foreign form of address.

A certainty grew in his brain that it was "that same cursed man!"

He watched her face as she read it, and noticed the look of relief, as she, quite unconscious of his presence, absently spread the paper out, and his eyes caught the signature "Mimo" before he was aware of it.

"Mimo!" That was the brute's name.

And what could he say or do? They were not really husband and wife, and as long as she did nothing to disgrace the Tancred honour, he had no valid reason for questions or complaints.

Zara, comforted by the telegram, "Much better again today," had leisure to return to the subject which had lately begun to unconsciously absorb her, the subject of her lord!

She wondered what made him look so stern. His nobly cut face looked as if it were carved in stone. Just from an abstract artistic point of view, she told herself, she honestly admired him and his type.

It was finer than what any other race could produce, and she was glad that she too was half English. The lines were so slender, and yet so strong, and every bone balanced, and the look of superb health and athletic strength.

Suddenly, an intense quiver of unknown emotion rushed over her.

But the moment passed, and finally they got out of the train at Charing Cross, after an unremarkable wedding journey.

* * *

Francis Markrute's moral antennae, upon which he prided himself, informed him that all was not as it should be between this young bride and groom.

Zara seemed to have acquired in this short

week an even extra air of regal dignity, aided by her perfect clothes, and Tristram looked stern and less joyous and more haughty than he had done.

But they were both so deadly cold! Cold, and certainly constrained. It was not one of the financier's habits ever to doubt himself or his deductions. They were based upon far too sound reasoning.

No, if something had gone wrong, or had not yet evolutionised, it was only for the moment, and need cause no philosophical *deus ex machina,* no uneasiness.

Meanwhile, it was his business, as the friend and uncle of the two, to be genial and make things run smoothly.

"By George, my dear boy," the financier said, "I dont believe I ever realised what a gorgeously beautiful creature my niece is. She is like some wonderful exotic blossom, a mass of snow and flame!"

"Certainly snow, but where is the flame?" Tristram replied, with unconscious cynicism.

Francis Markrute looked at him out of the corners of his clever eyes. She had been no joy to him in Paris, then!

"In a year or so, when you and Zara have a son, I will give you some papers, my dear boy, to read, which will interest you, as showing the mother's side of his lineage. It will be a fit balance, as far as actual blood goes, to your own."

In a year or so, when Zara should have a son!

Of all the aspects of the case which her pride and disdain had robbed him of, this, Tristram felt, was perhaps the most cruel. He would have no son!

He got up suddenly and threw his unfinished cigar into the grate, and said, in a strained voice:

"That is good of you. I shall have to have it inserted in the family tree someday. But now I think I shall turn in. I want to have my eye rested and be as fit as a fiddle for the shoot. I have had a tiring week."

Francis Markrute came out with him into the passage and up to the first floor, and they heard the notes of the "Chanson Triste" being played from Zara's sitting-room.

"Good God!" said Tristram. "I don't know why, but I wish to heaven she would not play that tune."

"Go and take her to bed," the financier suggested. "Perhaps she does not like being left alone so long."

Tristram went up the stairs with a bitter laugh to himself.

He did not go near the sitting-room; he went straight into the room which had been allotted to him. And a savage sense of humiliation and impotent rage convulsed him.

* * *

The next day, the Express which would stop for them at Tylling Green, the little station for Montfitchet, started at two o'clock. And the financier had given orders to have an early lunch at twelve, before they left.

He himself went off to the City at ten o'clock. He read his letters, and was surprised, when he asked Turner if Lord and Lady Tancred had breakfasted, to hear that Her Ladyship had gone out at half past nine and that His Lordship had given orders to his valet not to disturb him.

"See that they have everything they want," he said and left.

But when he was in his electric brougham, gliding eastwards, he frowned to himself.

"The proud little minx! So she has insisted upon keeping to the business bargain up till now, has she!" he thought. "If it goes on, we shall have to make her jealous. That would be an infallible remedy for her caprice."

But Zara was not concerned with such things at all for the moment. She was waiting anxiously for Mimo in the British Museum, and he was late. He would have the latest news of Mirko. No reply had awaited her, from her telegram to Mrs Morley from Paris, and it had been too late to wire again last night.

Someday, she hoped, when she could grow perhaps more friendly with her husband, she would get her uncle to let her tell him about Mirko.

It would make everything so much more simple, with regard to seeing him, and why, since the paper was all signed and nothing could be altered, should there be any mystery now?

Yet, only the day before the wedding her uncle had said:

"I beg of you not to mention the family disgrace of your mother to your husband, nor to speak to him of the man Sykypri, for a long time."

Francis Markrute had reasoned to himself, if the boy dies, as Morley thinks there is every likelihood, why should Tristram ever know?

The disgrace of his adored sister always made him wince.

Mimo came at last, looking anxious and haggard, but he told her Mirko was better, decidedly better, the attack had again been very short. So she felt reassured for the moment.

When it was past eleven o'clock, Zara returned quickly to Park Lane, and was coming in at the door just as her husband was descending the stairs.

"You are up very early, Milady," he said casually, and because of the servants in the hall, she felt it would look better to follow him into the library.

Tristram felt surprised at this, and he longed to ask her where she had been.

"What time do we arrive at your uncle's? Is it five or six?" she asked.

"It only takes three hours. We shall be there

about five. And, Zara, I want you to wear the sable coat. I think it suits you better than the chinchilla you had when we left."

She flushed a little. This was the first time he had ever spoken of her clothes; and to hide the sudden strange emotion she felt, she said coldly:

"Yes, I intended to. I shall always hate that chinchilla coat."

He turned away to the window, stung again by her words, which she had said unconsciously. The chinchilla had been her conventional "going-away" bridal finery. That was, of course, why she hated the remembrance of it.

As soon as she had said the words she felt sorry. What on earth made her wound him so often?

He stayed with his back turned, looking out the window, so, after waiting a moment, she left the room.

At the station they found Jimmy Danvers and a Mr and Mrs Harcourt, with her sister Miss Opie, and several men. The rest of the party, including Emily and Mary, Jimmy told them, had gone down by the eleven o'clock train.

Both Mrs Harcourt and her sister, and, indeed, the whole company, were Tristram's old and intimate friends, and they were so delighted to see him. They chaffed him and were gay, and only Zara was a stranger and out in the cold.

After a while the party arranged themselves, some to play bridge and some for sleep. Jimmy

Danvers and Colonel Lowerby went into the small compartment to smoke.

"Well, Crow," said Jimmy, "what do you think of Tristram's new lady? Isn't she a wonder? But Jehoshaphat! doesn't she freeze you to death!"

"Very curious type," growled the Crow. "Bit of Vesuvius underneath, I expect."

"Yes, that is what a fellow'd think to look at her," Jimmy said, puffing at his cigarette. "But she keeps the crust on the top all the time; the bloomin' volcano don't get a chance!"

"She doesn't look stupid," continued the Crow. "She looks stormy; expect it's pretty well worthwhile, though, when she melts."

"Poor old Tristram don't look as if he had had a taste of Paradise, does he? Before we'd heartened him up on the platform a bit, give you my word, he looked as glum as an owl," Jimmy said.

"And she looks like an iceberg," he went on after a moment, "as she's done all the time. I've never seen her once warm up."

"He's awfully in love with her," grunted the Crow.

"I believe that is about the measure, though I can't see how you've guessed it. You did not get back for the wedding, Crow, and it don't show now."

"Oh, doesn't it!" he said.

"Well, tell me, what do you really think of

her?" Jimmy went on. "You see, I was best man at the wedding, and I feel in a way responsible if she is going to make the poor old boy awfully unhappy."

"She's unhappy herself," said the Crow. "It's because she is unhappy she's so cold."

"Lady Highford's going to be at Montfitchet," Jimmy announced after a pause. "She won't make things easy for anyone, will she?"

"How did that happen?" asked the Crow in an astonished voice.

"Ethelrida had asked her in the Season, when everyone supposed the affair was still on, and I expect that she would not let them put her off...."

And then both men looked up at the door, for Tristram peeped in.

"We shall be arriving in five minutes," he informed them.

There were motor-cars and an omnibus to meet them when they arrived at the station, and Lady Ethelrida's own comfortable coupe for the bridal pair.

They might just want to say a few words together alone, before arriving, she had thought kindly.

Zara felt excited. She was beginning to realise that these English people were all of her dead father's class, not creatures whom one must beware of, until one knew whether or not they were gamblers or rogues.

It made her breathe more freely, and the black panther's look died out of her eyes. She did not feel nervous, as she well might have done; only excited and highly worked up.

Tristram, for his part, wished to heaven that Ethelrida had not arranged to send the coupe for them. It was such a terrible temptation for him to resist her, in the dusk of the afternoon!

He clenched his hands under the rug, and drew as far away from her as he could, and she glanced at him and wondered, almost timidly, why he looked so stern.

"I hope you will tell me if there is anything special you wish me to do, please," she said. "Because, you see, I have never been in the English country before, and . . . and my uncle has given me to understand the customs are different from those abroad."

He felt he could not look at her, the unusual gentleness in her voice was so alluring, but he could forget the hurt of the chinchilla coat. If he relented in his attitude at all, she would certainly snub him again; so he continued staring in front of him, and answered ordinarily:

"I expect you will do everything perfectly right, and everyone will only want to be kind to you, and make you have a good time; and my uncle will certainly make love to you, but you must not mind that."

"No, I shall not in the least object to that!" Zara smiled.

He could see out of the corner of his eye that she was smiling, and the temptation to clasp her to him was so overpowering that he said rather hoarsely:

"Do you mind if I put the window down?"

He must have some air; he was choking. And she wondered more and more what was the matter with him, and they both fell into a constrained silence, which lasted until they turned into the park gates.

The house was very enormous and stately, and, walking with her empress air, they at last came to the picture gallery, where the rest of the party who had arrived earlier were all assembled in the centre, with their host and hostess, having tea.

The Duke and Lady Ethelrida came forward down the very long, narrow room, and then when they did, they both kissed Zara, their beautiful new relation!

Lady Ethelrida, taking her arm, drew her towards the party, while she whispered:

"You, dear, lovely thing. Ever so many welcomes to the family and Montfitchet."

Zara suddenly felt a lump in her throat. How she had misjudged them all in her hurt ignorance! And determining to repair her injustice, she advanced with a smile and was presented to the group.

Chapter
Five

Tristram was ready for dinner in good time, but he hesitated about knocking at his wife's door. If she did not let him know she was ready, he would send Higgins to ask for her maid.

His eyes were shining with the pride he felt in her. He had not believed it possible that she could have been so gracious, and he had not even guessed that she would condescend to speak so much.

All his old friends had been so awfully nice about her, and honestly admiring, except Arthur Elterton, who had admired her rather too much!

And then his exaltation died down. It was, after all, but a very poor outside show, when in reality he could not even knock at her door!

He wished now he had never let his pride hurl forth that ultimatum on the wedding night, because he would have to stick to it! He could not make the slightest advance, and it did not look as if she meant to do so.

Zara, at the other side of the door, felt almost happy. It was the first evening in her life she had ever dressed without some heavy burden of care.

Her self-protective, watchful instincts could rest for a while; these new relations were truly so kind.

The only person she immediately and instinctively disliked was Lady Highford, who had gushed, and said one or two bittersweet things, which she had not clearly or literally understood, but which, she felt, were meant to be hostile.

It was plain to be seen that everyone loved her husband, from the old Duke, to the old setter by the fire. And how was it possible for them all to love a man, when, and then her thoughts unconsciously turned to "if," he were capable of so base a thing as his marriage with her had been?

Was it possible there could be any mistake?

On the first opportunity she would question her uncle; and although she knew that gentleman would only tell her exactly as much as he wished her to know, that much would be the truth.

Dinner was to be at half past eight. She ought to be punctual, she knew; but it was all so wonderful and refined and old-world, in her charming room, that she felt inclined to dawdle and look round.

Then she roused herself. She *must* dress. Fortunately her hair did not take any time to twist up.

"Milady is a dream!" Henriette exclaimed when at last she was ready. "Milord will be proud!"

And he was.

She sent Henriette to knock at his door, his door in the passage, not the one between their rooms, just on the stroke of half past eight. He was at that moment going to send Higgins on an errand! His sense of humour at the grotesqueness of the situation made him laugh, with a bitter laugh.

The two servants as the messengers! When he ought to have been in there himself, helping to fix on her jewels and playing with her hair, and perhaps kissing her exquisite shoulders, when the maid was not looking, or fastening on her dress!

He hardly allowed himself to tell her she looked very beautiful as they walked along the great corridor. She was in a deep sapphire-blue gauze, with no jewels on at all but the Duke's splendid brooch.

That was exquisite of her, he appreciated that fine touch. Indeed, he appreciated everything about her, if she had known.

People were always punctual in this house, and after the silent hush of admiration caused by the bride's entrance, they all began talking and laughing.

As Zara walked along the white drawing-room, on the old Duke's arm, she felt that somehow she had got back to a familiar atmosphere, where she was at rest, after long years of strife.

Lady Ethelrida had gone in with the bride-groom, and on her left hand she had placed the bride's uncle.

And Francis Markrute, as he looked round the table, with the perfection of its taste, and saw how everything was so beautiful, felt he had been justified in his schemes.

Lady Anningford sat beyond Tristram, and often the two talked, so Lady Ethelrida had plenty of time, without neglecting him, to converse with her other interesting guest.

"I am so glad you like our old home, Mr Markrute," she said. "Tomorrow I will show you a number of my favourite haunts."

"I shall be delighted," he replied, and they talked gaily together for the rest of the dinner.

* * *

In the white drawing-room afterwards, Lady Highford was particularly gushing to the new bride. She came with a group of other women to surround her.

"Your husband and I are such very dear old friends. And how lovely it is to think that now he will be able to reopen Wrayth! Dear Lady Tancred is so glad," she purred.

Zara just looked at her politely. "What a done-up ferret woman!" she thought.

"I have never heard my husband speak of you," she said, presently, when she had silently borne a good deal of vitriolic gush. "You have perhaps been out of England for some time?"

When the men came in, Tristram deliberately found Laura, who had moved away from Zara, and sat down upon a distant sofa with her, and Zara suddenly felt some unpleasant feeling about her heart.

She found that she desired to watch them, and that, in spite of what anyone said to her, her attention wandered back to the distant sofa, in some unconscious speculation and unrest.

Laura was being exceedingly clever. She scented, with the cunning of her species, that Tristram was really unhappy, whether he was in love with his hatefully beautiful wife or not.

Now was her chance, not by reproaches, but by sympathy, and if possible by planting in his heart some venom towards his wife.

"Tristram, dear, why did you not tell me? Did you not know I would have been delighted at anything if it pleased you?"

She looked down and sighed.

"I always made it my pleasure to understand you, and to promote whatever seemed for your good."

"You are a dear, Laura," he said, in a surprised voice.

"And now you must tell me if you are really happy, Tristram. She is so lovely, your wife, but looks very cold. And, I know . . ."

She hesitated.

"I know you don't like women to be cold."

"We will not discuss my wife," he said. "Tell me what you have been doing, Laura. Let me see, when did I see you last? In June?"

"Yes, in June," she said sadly, turning her eyes down. "And you might have told me, Tristram. It came as such a sudden shock. It made me seriously ill. You must have known, and were probably engaged, even then."

Tristram sat mute, for how could he announce the truth?

"Oh, don't let us talk of these things, Laura. Let us forget those old times and begin again differently. You will be a dear friend to me always, I am sure. You always were."

He stopped abruptly. He felt this was too much lying! And he hated doing such things.

"Of course I will, dar . . . Tristram," Laura said, and appeared much moved.

From where Zara was trying to talk to the Duke, she saw the woman quiver, and look down provokingly. A sudden unknown sensation of blinding rage came over her, and she did not hear a syllable of the Duke's speech.

* * *

"And you will really show me your favourite haunts tomorrow, Lady Ethelrida?" Francis Markrute was saying to his hostess.

He had contrived insidiously to detach her conversation from a group to himself, and drew her unconsciously towards a seat where they would be uninterrupted.

Lady Ethelrida never spoke of herself, as a rule. She was not in the habit of getting into those thrilling conversations with men, which most of the modern young women delighted in.

It was because, for some unacknowledged reason, the financier personally pleased her, that she now drifted where he wished.

"Zara looks very lovely tonight," she said.

"Yes," replied the financier, which was indeed what he felt. "And I hope someday they will be exceedingly happy."

"Why do you say someday?" Lady Ethelrida asked quickly. "I hoped they were happy now."

"Not very, I am afraid," he said. "But you remember our compact at dinner? They will be ideally so if they are left alone."

He glanced casually at Tristram and Laura.

Ethelrida looked too, following his eyes.

"Yes," she said. "I wish I had not asked her . . ." and then she stopped abruptly, and grew a deep pink.

She realised what the inference in her speech was, and if Mr Markrute had never heard anything about the silly affair between her cousin and Lady Highford, what would he think! What might she not have done!

"That won't matter," he said, with his fine smile. "It will be good for my niece. I meant something quite different."

133

But what he meant he would not say.

The evening passed smoothly. The girls and all the young men and the Crow, and young Billy, and giddy, irresponsible people like that, had gathered at one end of the room. They were arranging some special picnic for the morrow, as only some of them were going to shoot.

Into their picnic plans they drew Zara, and barred Tristram out with chaff.

"You are only an old married man now, Tristram," they teased him. "But Lady Tancred is young and comes with us!"

"And I will take care of her," announced Lord Elterton, looking sentimental, much to Tristram's disgust.

"Lady Thornby and Lady Melton and Lily Opie and her sister are going out to the shooters' lunch," Laura said sweetly. "As you are going to be deprived of your lovely wife, Tristram, I will come too."

Finally, good-nights were said, and the ladies retired to their rooms, and Zara could not think why she no longer found the atmosphere of hers peaceful and delightful, as she had done before she went down.

For the first time in her life she felt she hated a woman!

Tristram, when he came up an hour or so later, wondered if she was asleep. Laura had been perfectly sweet, and he felt greatly soothed. Poor old Laura!

He supposed she had really cared for him, and perhaps he had behaved rather casually, even though she had been impossible in the past.

But how had he ever fancied himself, even for five minutes, in love with her? Why, she looked quite old tonight! and he had never remarked before how thin and fluffed out her hair was. Women ought certainly to have beautiful thick hair.

Then all the pretences of any healing of his aches fell from him, and he went and stood by the door that separated him from his loved one, and he stretched out his arms and said aloud:

"Darling, if only you could understand how happy I would make you, if you would let me! But I can't even break down this hateful door, which I want to, because of my vow."

* * *

The next day did not look at all promising as regarded the weather, but still the shooters, Tristram among them, started early for their sport.

After the merriest breakfast, at little tables, in the great dining-room, the intending picnickers met in conclave, to decide what they should do.

"It is perfectly sure to rain," Jimmy Danvers said. "There is no use attempting to go to Lynton Heights. Why don't we take the lunch to Montfitchet Tower, and eat it in the big hall? There we wouldn't get wet."

"Quite right, Jimmy," agreed the Crow, who, with Lady Anningford, was to chaperon the young fold. "I'm all for not getting wet, with my rheumatic shoulder, and I hear you and young Billy are a couple of first-class cooks."

"Then," interrupted Lady Betty enthusiastically, "we can cook our own lunch! Oh, how delightful! We will make a fire in the big chimney. Uncle Crow, you are a pet!"

"I will go and give orders for everything at once," Lady Ethelrida agreed delightfully. "Jimmy, what a bright boy to have thought of the plan!"

By twelve o'clock all was arranged. It had been settled the night before, that Mr Markrute should shoot with the Duke and the rest of the more serious men.

However, early in the morning that astute financier had sent a note to His Grace's room, saying, if it were not putting out the guns dreadfully, he would crave to be excused.

He was expecting a telegram of the gravest importance, concerning the new Turkish loan, which he would be obliged to answer by special letter, and he was uncertain at what time the wire would come.

He was extremely sorry, but, he added whimsically, the Duke must remember he was only a poor businessman.

His Grace had smiled as he thought of his guest's vast millions, in comparison to his own fortune.

Thus it was that just before twelve o'clock, when the young party were ready to start for

their picnic, he, having written his letter and
despatched it by express to London, chanced upon Lady Ethelrida, in a place where he felt sure
he should find her.

He expressed his surprise that they were not
already gone, and he begged to be allowed to
come with them. He, too, was an excellent cook,
he assured her, and would be really of use. And
they all laughingly started.

If she could have seen the important letter
concerning the new Turkish loan, she would have
found it contained a pressing reminder to Bom-
pus to send down that night certain exquisitely
bound books!

* * *

Zara, who walked demurely by Lord Elterton, had never seen anything like this before.
She felt like a little child at her first party.

Lord Elterton had already fallen in love. He
was a true *cavaliere servante;* he knew, like the
financier, as a fine art how to manipulate the
temperaments of most women. He prided himself upon it.

Indeed, he spent the greater part of his life
doing nothing else.

Though Lady Tancred had been married only
a week, he hoped to render her not quite indifferent to himself in some way. He had seen at
once that she and Tristram were not on terms of
passionate love, and there was something so
piquant about flirting with the bride!

"You have not been long in this country, Lady Tancred, have you?" he said. "One can see it, you are so exquisitely *chic*. And how perfectly you speak English! Not the slightest accent. It is delicious. Did you learn it very young?"

"My father was an Englishman," said Zara, disarmed from her usual chilling reserve, by the sympathy in his voice. "It is a nice honest language."

"You speak other languages, probably?" Lord Elterton went on admiringly.

"Yes, four or five. It is very easy when one is moving in the countries, and certain languages are very much alike."

"How clever you are!"

"No, I am not a bit. But I have had time to read a good deal . . ."

Zara stopped. It was so against her habit to give personal information like this to anyone.

Lord Elterton saw the little check, and went on another tack.

"I have been an idle fellow, and am not at all learned," he said. "Tristram and I were at Eton together in the same house, and we were both dunces; but he did rather well at Oxford, and I went straight into the Guards."

Zara longed to ask about Tristram. She had not heard before that he had even been to Oxford! And it struck her suddenly how ridiculous the whole thing was.

She had sold herself for a bargain; she had

asked no questions of anyone: she had intended
to despise the whole family and remain entirely
aloof, and now she found every one of her inten-
tions being gradually upset.

But, as yet, she did not admit for a second
to herself that she was falling in love.

Montfitchet Tower was all that remained of
the old castle, destroyed by Cromwell's Iron-
sides. It was just one large long room, a sort
of great hall. It had stood roofless for many years,
and then been covered in by the old Duke's father, and contained a splendid stone chimney-
piece of colossal proportions.

And on a wet day it was an ideal picnic
place, and a bright wood fire was already blazing.

After lunch, which had been carried through
with all the proper ceremonies of the olden time,
it came on to pour with rain, so they decided that
the mediaeval dances should begin.

Accordingly they turned on the Gramo-
phone, which stood in the corner.

Gradually something of the excitement of
the gay young spirits spread to her, and she forgot her sorrows, and began to enjoy herself.

"I have brought you down the book we spoke
of, you know; and you will take it from me, won't
you, just as a remembrance of this day, and how
you made me young for an hour?"

They stopped by one of the benches at the
side and sat down, and Lady Ethelrida answered
softly:

"Yes, if . . . you wish me to. . . ."

Zara was dancing with Lord Elterton. His whole bearing was one of intense devotion, and she was actually laughing, and looking up into his face, still affected by the general hilarity, when the door opened and some of the shooters peeped into the room.

It had been too impossibly wet to go on, and they had sent the ladies back in the motors, and had come across the park, on their way home, and, hearing the sound of music, had glanced in.

Tristram was in front of the intruders, and just chanced to catch his bride's look at her partner, before either of them saw they were observed.

He felt frightfully jealous. He had never before seen her so smiling, to begin with, and never at himself.

He longed to kick Arthur Elterton! Confounded impertinence! And what nonsense dancing like this in the afternoon, with boots on!

When they all stopped, and greeted the shooters, and crowded round the fire, he said in a tone of rasping sarcasm, in reply to Jimmy Danvers's announcement that they were back in the real life of a castle in the Middle Ages:

"Anyone can see that! You have got even My Lady's fool. Look at Arthur with mud on his boots, jumping about!"

Lord Elterton felt very flattered. He knew

his old friend was jealous, and if he was jealous, then the charming cold lady must have been unbelievably nice to him, and that meant he was getting on!

"You are jealous because your lovely bride prefers me, Young Lochinvar," and he laughed as he quoted:

"'For so faithful in love and so dauntless in war—
There ne'er was a gallant like Young Lochinvar!'"

Zara saw that Tristram's eyes flashed blue-steel, and that he did not like the chaff at all.

He had been with Lady Highford all day, so why should she not amuse herself too, indeed, why should either of them care what the other did?

So just out of wilfulness, she smiled again at Lord Elterton, and said:

"'Then tread we a measure, my Lord Lochinvar.'"

And off they went.

Tristram, with his face more set than the Crusader ancestor's in Wrayth Church, said to his uncle, Lord Charles:

"We are all wet through. Let us come along." He turned round and went out.

As he walked, he wondered to himself how much she must know of English poetry, to have been able to answer Arthur like that. If only

141

they could be friends, and talk of the books he too loved!

He felt he was getting to the end of his tether; it could not go on. Her words that night at Dover had closed down all the possible sources he could have used for her melting.

And a man cannot, in a week, break through a thousand years of inherited pride.

When he had left, although she would not own it to herself, Zara's joy in the day was gone. The motors came to fetch them presently, and they all went back to the castle, to dress and have tea.

Tristram's face was still stony, and he had sat down in a sofa by Laura, when a footman brought a telegram to Zara. He watched her open it, with concentrated interest. From whom were these mysterious telegrams?

He saw her face change as it had done in Paris, only not so seriously, and then she crushed up the paper into a ball, and threw it in the fire. The telegram had been:

"Very slightly feverish again," and signed "Mimo."

"Now I remember where I have seen your wife before!" said Laura.

"Where?" Tristram said absently.

"In the waiting room at Waterloo Station, and yet, no, it could not have been she; because she was quite ordinarily dressed, and she was talking very interestedly to a foreign man."

She watched Tristram's face, and saw she had hit home for some reason, so she went on, enchanted:

"Of course it could not have been she, naturally; but the type is so peculiar that any other like it would remind one, would it not?"

"I expect so," he said. "It could not have been Zara, though, because she was in Paris until just before the wedding."

"I remember the occasion quite well. It was the day after the engagement was announced. because I had been up for Flora's wedding, and was going down into the country."

Then, in a flash, it came to him that that was the very day he himself had seen Zara in Whitehall, the day when she had not gone to Paris.

And rankling, uncomfortable suspicions overcame him again.

Laura felt delighted. She did not know why he should be moved at her announcement, but he certainly was, so it was worthwhile rubbing it in.

"Has she a sister, perhaps? Because now I come to think of it, the resemblance is extraordinary. I remember I was rather interested at the time, because the man was so awfully handsome, and, as you know, I have always had a passion for handsome men!"

"My wife was an only child," Tristram answered.

What was Laura driving at?

"Well, she has a double, then," she laughed.

"I watched them for quite ten minutes, so I am sure. I was waiting for my maid, who was to meet me, and I could not leave for fear of missing her."

"How interesting!" said Tristram coldly.

He would not permit himself to demand a description of the man.

"Perhaps after all it was she, before she went to Paris, and I may be mistaken about the date," Laura went on. "It might have been her brother; he was certainly foreign, but no, it could not have been a brother."

She looked down and smiled knowingly.

Tristram felt gradually wild with the stings her words were planting, and then his anger rebounded upon herself. Little natures always miscalculate the effect of their actions and so they miss their ultimate ends.

Laura only longed, after hurting Tristram as a punishment, to get him back again; but she was not clever enough to know that to make him mad with jealousy about his wife was not the way.

"I don't understand what you wish to insinuate, Laura," he said, in a contemptuous voice; "but whatever it is, it is having no effect upon me. I absolutely adore my wife, and know everything she does, or does not do."

"Oh! the poor, angry darling, there, there!" she laughed, spitefully, "and was it jealous! Well, it shan't be teased. But what a clever husband, to know all about his wife! He should be put in a glass case in a museum!"

And she got up and left him alone.

Tristram would have liked to kill someone, he did not know whom, this foreign man, "Mimo," most likely. He had not forgotten the name!

Now, if the evening passed with pain and unrest for the bride and bridegroom, it had quite another aspect for Francis Markrute and Lady Ethelrida!

He was not placed by his hostess tonight at dinner, but when the power of manipulating circumstances with skill is in a man, and the desire to make things easy to be manipulated is in a woman, they can spend agreeable and numerous moments together.

So without any apparent or pointed detachment from her other guests, Lady Ethelrida was able to sit in one of the embrasures of the windows in the picture gallery, whither the party had migrated tonight, and talk to her interesting new friend.

He seemed so wonderfully understanding, and was so quiet, and subtle, and undemonstrative, and underneath you could feel his power and strength.

She told him in detail all about Wrayth.

"It sounds wonderful," said the financier.

"Lots of it is very shabby, of course, because Tristram's father was always very hard up, and nothing had been done much either, in the grandfather's time, except the horrible wing.

"But with enough money to get it right again,

145

I cannot imagine anything more lovely than it could be."

"It will be a great amusement to them in the coming year to do it all, then," Francis Markrute said. "Zara has the most beautiful taste, Lady Ethelrida. When you know her better, I think you will like my niece."

"But I do now," she exclaimed. "Only I do wish she did not look so sad."

She paused with gentle timidity.

"Will you tell me why? Do you know of any special reason today to make her unhappy? I saw her face at dinner tonight, and all the while she talked, there was an anxious, hunted look in her eyes."

Francis Markrute frowned for a moment, he had been too absorbed in his own interests to have taken in anything special about his niece. If there was something of the sort in her eyes, it could only have one source, anxiety about the health of the boy, Mirko.

He himself had not heard anything. Then his lightning calculations decided him to tell Lady Ethelrida nothing of this. Zara's anxiety would mean the child's illness, and illness, Dr Morley had warned him, could have only one end.

He wished the poor little fellow no harm, but on the other hand, he had no sentiment about him. If he was going to die, then the disgrace would be wiped away, and need never be spoken about.

"There is something which troubles her now and then. It will pass presently. Take no notice of it," he answered slowly.

So Lady Ethelrida, as mystified as ever, changed the conversation.

"May I give you the book tomorrow morning before we go to shoot?" the financier asked after a moment. "It is your birthday, I believe, and all your guests on that occasion are privileged to lay some offering at your feet."

He paused.

"I wanted to do so this afternoon, after tea, but I was detained playing bridge with your father. I have several books coming tomorrow that I do so want you to have."

"It is very kind of you. I would like to show you my sitting-room, in the south wing. Then you could see that they would have a comfortable home!"

"When may I come?"

This was direct, and Lady Ethelrida felt a piquant sensation of interest. She had never in her life made an assignation with a man.

"You breakfast downstairs at half past nine, like this morning?"

"Yes, I always do, and the girls will, and almost everyone, because it will be my birthday."

"Then if I come exactly at half past ten, will you be there?"

"I will try."

Lady Ethelrida experienced a distinct feeling of excitement over this innocent rendezvous.

Meanwhile, Lord Elterton was losing no time in his pursuit of Zara. He had been among the first to leave the dining-room, several paces in front of Tristram and the others, and instantly came to her, and suggested a tour of the pictures.

Zara, thankful to divert her mind, went with him willingly, and soon found herself standing in front of an immense portrait of himself given by the Regent to the Duke's grandfather, one of his great friends.

"I have been watching you all through dinner," Lord Elterton said, "and you looked like a beautiful storm, your dress the grey, and your eyes the threatening thunder-clouds."

"One feels like a storm sometimes," said Zara.

"People are so tiresome as a rule, you can see through them in half an hour. But no one could ever guess about what you are thinking."

"No one would want to, if they knew."

"Is it so terrible as that?"

He smiled, she must be diverted.

"I wish I had met you long ago, because, of course, I cannot tell you all the things I now want to; Tristram would be so confoundedly jealous, like he was this afternoon. It is the way of husbands."

Zara did not reply. She quite agreed to this, for the jealousy of husbands she had experience!

"Now, if I were married," Lord Elterton went on, "I would try to make my wife so happy, and would love her so much, she would never give me cause to be jealous."

"Love!" said Zara. "How you talk of love, and what does it mean? Gratification to oneself, or to the loved person?"

"Both," said Lord Elterton, and looked down so devotedly into her eyes, that the old Duke, who was near with Laura, thought it was quite time the young man's innings should be over.

So he joined them.

"Come with me, Zara, while I show you some of Tristram's ancestors, on his mother's side."

He placed her arm in his gallantly, and led her away to the most interesting pictures.

"Well, 'pon my soul!" he said, as they went along. "Things are vastly changed since my young days. Here, Tristram."

He beckoned to his nephew, who was with Lady Anningford.

"Come here and help me to show your wife some of your forebears."

Then he went on with his original speech.

"Yes, as I was saying, things are vastly changed since I brought Ethelrida's dear mother back here, after our honeymoon, a month in those days!

"I would have punched any other young blood's head, who had even looked at her! And you philander off with that fluffy little empty-pate, Laura, and Arthur Elterton makes love to your bride! A pretty state of things, 'pon my soul!"

He laughed reprovingly.

Tristram smiled with bitter sarcasm as he answered:

"You are absurdly old-fashioned, Uncle. But perhaps Aunt Corisande was different from the modern woman."

Zara did not speak.

"Oh, you must not ever blame the women," the Duke said. "If they are different, it is the fault of the men. I took care that my Duchess wanted me! Why, my dear boy, I was jealous of even her maid, for at least a year!"

Tristram thought to himself that he went further than that, and was jealous of even the air Zara breathed!

"You must have been awfully happy, Uncle," he said with a sigh.

But Zara spoke never a word. But the Duke saw that there was something too deeply strained between them for his kindly meant persiflage to do any good.

He changed the conversation into lighter subjects.

* * *

When finally everyone had retired for the night, Zara did not attempt to get into her bed, after she had dismissed her maid. She sat down in one of the big armchairs, and clasped her hands tightly, and tried to think.

Things were coming to a crisis with her. Destiny had given her another cross to bear, for suddenly this evening, as the Duke spoke of his wife, she had become conscious of the truth about herself, she was in love with her husband.

And she herself had made it impossible that he could ever come back to her. For indeed the tables were turned, with one of those ironical twists of Fate.

Why did she love him? She had reproached him on her wedding night, when he had told her he loved her, because, in her ignorance, she felt then that it could only be a question of the senses.

She had called him an animal, she remembered, and now she had become an animal herself! For she could prove no loftier motive for her emotion towards him than that which he had had for her then; they knew each other no better.

They were strangers to each other still, and yet this cruel, terrible thing, called love, had broken down all the barriers in her heart, melted the disdainful ice, and turned it to fire.

She felt she wanted to caress him, and take away the stern, hard look from his face. She wanted to be gentle and soft and loving, to feel that she belonged to him.

She passionately longed for him to kiss her and clasp her to his heart. Whether he had consented originally to marry her for her uncle's money or not was now a matter of no further importance.

He had loved her after he had seen her, at all events; and she had thrown it all away, nothing remained but a man's natural jealousy of his possessions.

"Oh, why did I not know what I was doing!" she moaned to herself. "I must have been very wicked in some former life, to be so tortured in this!"

But it was too late now; she had burnt her ships, and nothing remained to her but her pride. Since she had thrown away joy, she could at least keep that, and never let him see how she was being punished.

And tonight it was her turn to look in anguish at the closed door, and toss on her bed in restless pain of soul.

* * *

Almost everyone was punctual for breakfast. They all came in with their gifts for Lady Ethelrida, and there was much chaffing and joking, and delightful little shrieks of surprise, as the parcels were opened.

Nothing could have been more sweet and gracious than Her Ladyship was, and underneath her gentle heart was beating with an extra excitement when she thought of her rendezvous at half past ten o'clock!

Would he, she no longer thought of him as Mr Markrute, would he come to her sitting-room?

"I must go and give some orders now," she said, about a quarter past ten, to the group which surrounded her, when they had all got up, and were standing beside the fire. "And we assemble in the hall at eleven."

Francis Markrute, she noticed, had retired some moments before.

Lady Ethelrida stood looking out her window, in her fresh, white-panelled, lilac-chintzed bower. Her heart was actually thumping now.

Would he ever get away from her father, who seemed to have taken to having endless political discussions with him? Would he ever be able to come in time for a moment, before they must both go down?

She had taken the precaution to make herself quite ready to start, short skirt, soft felt hat, thick boots and all.

But as half past ten chimed from the Dresden clock on the mantelpiece, there was a gentle tap at the door, and Francis Markrute came in.

He knew in an instant, experienced fowler that he was, that his bird was fluttered with expectancy, and it gave him an exquisite thrill.

"You see, I have managed to come," he said softly, and he allowed something of the joy and tenderness he felt to come into his voice.

Lady Ethelrida answered a little nervously

153

that she was glad, and then continued quickly that she must show him her book-cases, because there was so little time.

"Only one short half hour, if you will let me stay so long," he pleaded.

In his hand he carried the original volume he had spoken about, a very old edition of Shakespeare's *Sonnets*. It was perfectly exquisitely bound and tooled, and had her monogram worked into a beautiful little medallion.

He handed it to her first.

"This I ventured to have ordered for you long ago," he said. "Six weeks it is nearly, and I so feared until yesterday that you would not let me give it to you. It is not meant for your birthday, it is our original bond of acquaintance."

"It is too beautiful," said Lady Ethelrida, looking down.

"And over there by your writing-table, you will find the books that are my birthday gift; if you will do me the delight of accepting them."

She went forward with a little cry of surprise and pleasure.

"How enchanting!" she said. "And look, they match my room. How could you have guessed . . . ?"

And then she broke off and again looked down.

"You told me the night I dined with you at Glastonbury House that you loved mauve as a colour, and that violets were your favourite flower. How could I forget?"

He then permitted himself to come a step nearer to her.

She did not move away. She turned over the leaves of the English volume rather hurriedly, the paper was superlatively fine, and the print a gem of art, and then she looked up, surprised.

"I have never seen this collection before," she said wonderingly. "All the things one loves, under the same cover!"

Then she turned to the title-page to see which edition it was, and she found that as far as information went, it was blank, and inscribed upon it in gold was simply:

To the Lady Ethelrida Montfitchet
From
F. M.

A deep pink flush rose on her delicate face, and she dared not raise her eyes.

"It will gratify me greatly if it has pleased you."

"Pleased me!" she said.

She looked up, for the sudden conviction came to her that to have this done took time, and a great deal of money. When could he have given the order? and what would this mean?

He read her thoughts.

"Yes," he said simply. "From the very first moment I ever saw you, Lady Ethelrida, to me you seemed all that was true and beautiful, the embodiment of my ideal of womanhood."

Ethelrida was so moved by some new sudden and exquisite emotion that she could not reply for a moment.

"It is too . . . too nice of you," she said softly, and there was a little catch in her breath. "No one has ever thought of anything so exquisite for me before, although, as you saw this morning, everyone is so very kind. How shall I thank you, Mr Markrute? I do not know."

"You must not thank me at all," he said. "And now I must tell you that the half hour is nearly up, and we must go down. But, may I, will you let me, come again, perhaps tomorrow afternoon?"

Ethelrida had also turned to look at the clock, She was too single-minded to fence now, or push this new strange joy out of her life, so she said:

"When the others go out for a walk, then, after lunch, yes, you may come."

* * *

Zara had at first thought she would not go out with the shooters. She felt numb, as if she could not pluck up enough courage to make conversation with anyone. She had received a letter from Mimo, by the second post, with the details of what he had heard of Mirko.

Agatha, the Morley's child, was to return home the following day, and Mirko had written an excited letter himself to announce this event, which Mimo enclosed.

He seemed perfectly well then, only at the end, as she would see, he had said he was dreaming of Maman every night. By this Mimo knew that it must mean that he was a little feverish again, so he had felt it wiser to telegraph.

Mirko had written out the score of the air Maman always came and taught him, and he was longing to play it to his dear papa, and his Cherisette.

She was just going up to her room at about a quarter to eleven, with the letter in her hand, when she met Tristram coming from his room, with his shooting boots on, ready to start.

He stopped and said coldly:

"You had better be quick putting your things on. My uncle always starts punctually."

Then his eye caught the foreign writing on the letter, and he turned brusquely away. She saw him turn away, and it angered her, in spite of her new mood. He need not show his dislike so plainly, she thought.

"I had not intended to come," she answered haughtily. "I am tired; and I do not know this sport, or if it will please me. I should feel for the poor birds, I expect."

"I am sorry you are tired," he answered, contrite in an instant. "Of course you must not come if you are. They will be awfully disappointed. But never mind. I will tell Ethelrida."

"It is nothing . . . my fatigue, I mean. If you think your cousin will mind, I will come."

She turned, without waiting for him to answer, and went on to her room.

Tristram, after going back to his for something he had forgotten, presently went on down the stairs, a bitter smile on his face, and at the bottom met Laura Highford.

She looked up into his eyes, and allowed tears to gather in hers. She had always plenty at her command.

"Tristram," she said with extreme gentleness, "you were cross with me yesterday afternoon, because you thought I was saying something about your wife.

"But don't you know, can't you understand, what it is to me to see you devoted to another woman? You may be changed, but I am always the same, and I . . . I . . ."

She buried her face in her hands and went into a flood of tears.

Tristram was overcome with confusion and horror. He loathed scenes. Good heavens, if anyone should come along!

"Laura, for goodness' sake. My dear girl, don't cry!" he exclaimed.

He felt he would say anything to comfort her, and get over the chance of someone seeing this hateful exhibition.

But she continued to sob. She had caught sight of Zara's figure on the landing above, and her vengeful spirit desired to cause trouble, even at a cost to herself.

Zara had been perfectly ready, all but her hat, and had hurried exceedingly to be in time, and thus had not been five minutes after her husband.

"Tristram!" wailed Laura, and, putting up her hands, placed them on his shoulders. "Darling, just kiss me once, quickly, to say good-bye."

It was at this stage that Zara came full upon them, from a turn in the stairs, and she heard Tristram say disgustedly, "No, I won't," and saw Lady Highford drop her arms.

In the three steps that separated them, her wonderful iron self-control, the inheritance of all her years of suffering, enabled her to stop as if she had seen nothing, and in an ordinary voice ask if they were to go to the great hall.

"The woman," as she called Laura, should not have the satisfaction of seeing a trace of emotion in her, or Tristram either.

He had answered immediately, "Yes," and had walked on by her side, in an absolutely raging temper.

How dared Laura drag him into a disgraceful and ridiculous scene like this! He could have wrung her neck. What must Zara think? That he was simply a cad!

He could not offer a single explanation, either; indeed, she had demanded none.

After a moment he blurted out:

"Lady Highford was very much upset about something, she is hysterical."

"Poor thing!" said Zara indifferently, and walked on.

But when they got into the hall where most of the company were, she suddenly felt her knees giving way under her, and hurriedly sank down on an oak chair.

She felt sick with jealous pain, even though she had plainly seen that Tristram was no willing victim. But upon what terms could they be, or have been, for Lady Highford so to lose all sense of shame!

Tristram was watching her anxiously. She must have seen the humiliating exhibition. He wished that she had reproached him or said something, anything, but to remain completely unmoved was too maddening.

Then the whole company, who were coming out, appeared, and they started. Some of the men were drawing lots to see if they should shoot in the morning or in the afternoon.

Zara walked by the Crow, who was not shooting at all. She was wearied with Lord Elterton, wearied with everyone.

"You have never seen your husband shoot yet, I expect, Lady Tancred, have you?" he asked her; and when she said, "No," he went on:

"Because you must watch him. He is a very fine shot."

She did not know anything about shooting, only that Tristram looked particularly attractive in his shooting clothes and that English sportsmen were natural, unceremonious creatures, whom she was beginning to like very much.

She wished she could open her heart to this quaint old man, and ask him to explain things to her; but she could not, and presently they got to a safe place and watched.

Tristram happened to be fairly near them, and, yes, he was a good shot, she could see that.

"Oh, that was wonderful!" she exclaimed, as Tristram got two rocketers at right and left, and then another with his second gun.

His temper had not affected his eye, it seemed.

"Tristram is one of the best all-round sportsmen I know," the Crow announced, "and he has got one of the kindest hearts. I have known him since he was a toddler."

Zara tried to control her interest.

"Are you looking forward to the reception at Wrayth on Monday? I always wonder how a person unaccustomed to England would view all the speeches and dinners, and the bonfire, and triumphal arches, and those things of a home-coming. Rather an ordeal, I expect."

Zara's eyes rounded, and she faltered.

"And shall I have to go through all that?"

The Crow was nonplussed. Had not her husband, then, told her what everyone else knew? Upon what possible terms could they be? And before he was aware of it, he had blurted out:

"Good Lord!"

Then the Crow turned the conversation, as they walked on to the next stand.

Did she know that Lady Ethelrida had commanded that all the ladies were to get up impromptu fancy dresses for tonight, her birthday dinner, and all the men would be in hunt-coats? he asked.

Large parties were coming from the only two other big houses near, and they would dance after in the picture gallery.

"A wonderful new band that came out in London this Season is coming down," he ended with.

As she replied that she had heard, he asked her what she intended to be.

"It must be something with your hair down, you must give us the treat of that!"

"I have left it all to Lady Ethelrida, and my sisters-in-law," she said. "We are going to contrive things the whole afternoon."

Chapter
Six

It was arranged that all the men, even the husbands, were to go down into the White Drawing-Room first, so that the ladies might have the pleasure of making an entrance.

When the group of Englishmen, being smart in their hunt-coats, were assembled at the end, by the fireplace, footmen opened the big double doors, and the groom of the chambers announced:

"Her Majesty Queen Guinevere, and the Ladies of her Court."

Ethelrida advanced, her fair hair in two long plaits and her mother's diamond crown upon her head. She wore a white brocade gown, under a blue merino cloak, trimmed with ermine and silver.

She looked perfectly regal, nearly beautiful, and to the admiring eyes of Francis Markrute she seemed to outshine all the rest.

Then, their names called as they entered, came:

"Enid" and "Elaine," each fair and sweet; and "Vivien" and "Ettarre"; then "Lynette" walking alone, with her saucy nose in the air, and her flaxen curls spread out over her cream robe, a most bewitching sight.

Several paces behind her came the "Three Fair Queens," all in wonderfully contrived garments, and misty, floating veils; and lastly, quite ten paces in the rear, walked "Isolt," followed by her "Brangaine."

And when the group by the fireplace caught sight of her, they one and all drew in their breath.

For Zara had surpassed all expectations. The intense and blatant blue of her long clinging robe seemed to enhance the beauty of her pure white skin and marvellous hair.

It fell like a red shining cloak all round her, kept in only by a thin fillet of gold, while her dark eyes gleamed with a new excitement.

She had relaxed her dominion of herself, and was allowing the natural triumphant woman in her to have its day. For once in her life she forgot everything of sorrow and care, and permitted herself to rejoice in her own beauty, and in its effect upon the world before her.

"Jehoshaphat!" was the first articulate word that the company heard, from the hush which had fallen upon them; and then there was a chorus of general admiration, in which all the ladies had their share.

Only the Crow happened to glance at Tristram, and saw that his face was white as death.

Then the two parties, about twenty people in all, began to arrive from the other houses, and delighted exclamations of surprise, at the splendour of the impromptu fancy garments, were heard all over the room, and soon dinner was announced, and they went in.

"My Lord Tristram," Ethelrida had said to her cousin, "I beg of you to conduct to my festal board your own most beautiful Lady Isolt. Remember! On Monday you leave us for the realm of King Mark, so make the most of your time!"

She turned and led Zara forward, and placed her hand in his.

He held his wife's hand until the procession started, and they neither spoke a word. Zara, still exalted with the spirit of the night, felt only a wild excitement.

She was glad he could see her beauty and her hair, and she raised her head and shook it back, as they started, with a provoking air.

But Tristram never spoke, and by the time they had reached the banqueting-hall some of her exaltation died down, and she felt a chill.

Her hair was so very long and thick that she had to push it aside to sit down, and in doing so a mesh flew out and touched his face.

The Crow, who was watching the whole drama intently, noticed that he shivered and, if possible, grew more pale.

So she turned to his own servant, behind his chair, who with some of the other valets was helping to wait, and whispered to him:

"Go and see that brandy is handed to Lord Tancred at once before the soup."

At last dessert-time came, with its toasts for the Queen Guinevere. And the bridal pair had not spoken a word to each other. Lady Anningford, who was watching them, began to fear for the success of her plan.

However, there was no use turning back now. So, amidst jests of all sorts in keeping with the spirit of Camelot and the Table Round, at last "Brangaine" rose and, taking the gold cup in front of her, said:

"I, Brangaine, commissioned by her Lady Mother to conduct the Lady Isolt safely to King Mark, under the knightly protection of the Lord Tristram, do now propose to drink the health, and yet must all do likewise, Lords and Ladies of Arthur's Court."

She sipped her own glass, while she handed the gold cup to the Duke, who passed it on to the pair; and Tristram, because all eyes were upon him, forced himself to continue the jest.

He rose, and taking Zara's hand, while he bowed to the company, gave her the cup to drink, and then took it himself, while he drained the measure.

And everyone cried, amidst great excitement.

"The health and happiness of Tristram and Isolt!"

Then, when the tumult had subsided a little, "Brangaine" gave a pretended shriek.

"Mercy me! I am undone!" she cried. "They have quaffed of the wrong cup! That gold goblet contained a love-potion, distilled from rare plants by the Queen, and destined for the wedding wine of Isolt and King Mark!

"And now the Lord Tristram and she have drunk it together by misadventure, and can never be parted more! Oh, misery me! What have I done!"

And amidst shouts of delighted laughter, led by the Crow, in frozen silence Tristram held his wife's hand.

But after a second, the breeding in them both, as on their wedding evening before the waiters, again enabled them to continue the comedy, and they too laughed, and, with the Duke's assistance, got through the rest of dinner.

If the cup had indeed contained a potion distilled by the Irish sorceress queen, the two victims could not have felt more passionately in love.

But Tristram's pride won the day for him, for this one time, and not by a glance or a turn of his head did he let his bride see how wildly her superlative attraction had kindled the fire in his blood.

When the dancing began he danced with every other lady first, and then went off into the smoking-room, and only just returned in time to be made to lead out his "Isolt" in a final quadrille, not a valse.

No powers would have made him endure the temptation of a valse!

* * *

The next afternoon, as Lady Ethelrida sat waiting for her guest, she looked absurdly young for her twenty-six years.

As the hour for the meeting chimed, Francis Markrute entered the room.

"This is perfectly divine," he said, as he came in, while the roguish twinkle of a schoolboy who has outwitted his mates sparkled in his fine eyes.

For about a quarter of an hour they talked of books. The daylight was drawing in, and they had an hour before them.

Slowly Francis Markrute told her all about himself, his dreams and ambitions.

"All his life," he went on, "from a boy's to a man's, this person we are speaking of had kept his ideal of the woman he should love. She must be fine and shapely, and noble and free, she must be tender and devoted, and gracious and good.

"But he passed all his early manhood, and grew to middle age, before he even saw her shadow across his path. He looked up one night, eighteen months ago, at a Court Ball, and she passed him on the arm of a Royal Duke, and unconsciously brushed his coat with her soft dove's wing.

"And he knew that it was she, after all those years. So he waited and planned, and met her once or twice, but fate did not let him advance very far, and so a scheme entered his head.

"His niece, the daughter of his dead sister, had also had a very unhappy life, and he thought she too should come among these English people and find happiness with their level ways.

"She was beautiful and proud and good, so he planned the marriage between his niece and the cousin of the lady he worshipped, knowing by that he should be drawn nearer his star, and also pay the debt to his dead sister by securing the happiness of her child.

"But primarily it was his desire to be nearer his own worshipped star, and thus it has all come about."

And then he paused and looked full at her face, and saw that her sweet eyes were moist with some tender, happy tears. So he leaned forward, and took her other hand and kissed them both, placing the soft palms against his mouth for a second.

Then he whispered hoarsely, his voice at last trembling with the passionate emotion which he felt:

"Ethelrida, darling, I love you with my soul. Tell me, my sweet lady, will you be my wife?"

Lady Ethelrida did not answer, but allowed herself to be drawn into his arms.

And so in the firelight, with the watchful grey owl, the two rested, blissfully content.

* * *

When Lady Ethelrida came down to tea, her sweet face was prettily flushed, for she was quite unused to caresses and the kisses of a man!

Her soft grey eyes were shining with a happiness of which she had not dreamed, and above all things she was filled with the exquisite emotion of having a secret!

Zara had not appeared at tea; she said she was very tired, and would rest until dinner. If she had been there, her uncle had meant to take her aside, into one of the smaller sitting-rooms, and tell her the piece of information he deemed it now advisable for her to know.

But as she did not appear, nor Tristram either, he thought after all they might be together, and his interference would be unnecessary, but he decided if he saw the same frigid state of things at dinner he would certainly speak to her after it.

And relieved from duty, he went once more to find his lady-love in her sitting-room.

Tristram had gone out for another walk alone. He wanted to realise the details of the coming week, and settle with himself how best to get through with them.

He and Zara were to start in their own motor at about eleven for Wrayth, which was only forty miles across the border, into Suffolk.

At the end of his troubled thoughts he had come to the conclusion that there was only one thing to be done: he must speak to her tonight, and tell her what to expect, and ask her to play her part.

"She is fortunately game, even if cold as a stone," he said to himself, "and if I appeal to her pride she will help me out."

So he came back into the house, and went straight up to her room.

He had been through too much suffering and anguish of heart, all night and all day, to be fearful of temptation; he felt numb as he knocked at the door, and an indifferent voice called out, "Come in."

He opened it a few inches, and said:

"It is I, Tristram. I have something I must say to you. May I come in? Or would you prefer to come down to one of the sitting-rooms? I daresay we could find one empty, so as to be alone."

"Please come in," she said, and she was conscious that she was trembling from head to foot.

She had been lying upon the sofa wrapped in a soft blue tea-gown, and her hair hung in the two long plaits which she always unwound when she could, to take its weight from her head.

She rose from her reclining position and sat in the corner, and after glancing at her for a second Tristram turned his eyes away, and leaning on the mantelpiece began in a cold grave voice:

"I have to ask you to do me a favour. It is to

171

help me through tomorrow, and the few days after, as best you can by conforming to our ways.

"It has been always the custom in the family, when a Tancred brought home his bride, to have all sorts of silly rejoicings. There will be triumphal arches in the park, and collections of village people, and then a lunch of principal tenants, and speeches, and all sorts of boring things.

"Then we shall have to dine alone in the State Dining-Room, with all the servants watching us, and then go to the household and tenants' ball in the great hall. It will all be ghastly, as you can see."

He paused a moment, but he did not change the set tone in his voice when he spoke again, nor did he look at her. He had now come to the hardest part of his task.

"All these people, who are my people," he went on, "think a great deal of these things, and of us, that is, myself, as their landlord, and you as my wife. We have always been friends, the country folk at Wrayth and my family, and they adored my mother.

"They are looking forward to us coming back and opening the house again, and . . ."

He paused again; it seemed as if his throat was dry, for suddenly the remembrance of his dreams as he looked at Tristram Guiscard's armour, which he had worn at Agincourt, came back to him, his dreams in his old oak-panelled room, of their home-coming to Wrayth; and the mockery of the reality hit him in the face.

He mastered the emotion which had hoarsened his voice, and went on in an even tone:

"What I have to ask is that you will do your share, wear some beautiful clothes, smile, look as if you cared, and if I feel that it will be necessary to take your hand, or even kiss you, do not frown at me, or think I am doing it from choice.

"I ask you, because I believe you are as proud as I am; I ask you, please, to play the game."

He looked up at her, but the terrible emotion she was suffering had made her droop her head. He would not kiss her, or take her hand, from choice! That was the main thing her woman's heart had grasped, the main thing, which cut her like a knife.

"You can count upon me," she said, so low he could hardly hear her.

Then she raised her head proudly, and looked straight in front of her, but not at him, while she repeated more firmly:

"I will do in every way what you wish, what your mother would have done. I am no weakling, you know, and as you said, I am as proud as yourself."

He dared not look at her, now that the bargain was made, so he took a step towards the door, and then turned and said:

"I thank you, I shall be grateful to you,

173

whatever may occur. Please believe that nothing that may look as if it was my wish to throw us together, as though we were really husband and wife, will be my fault.

"And you can count upon my making the thing as easy for you as I can, and when the mockery of the rejoicing is over, then we can discuss our future plans."

Although Zara was longing to cry aloud in passionate pain, "I love you, I love you! Come back and beat me if you will, only do not go coldly like that!" she never spoke a word, the strange iron habit of her life held her, and he went sadly from the room.

When he had gone, she could control herself no longer, and forgetful of coming maid and approaching dinner, she fell on the white bearskin rug before the fire, and gave way to passionate tears.

* * *

The last dinner at Montfitchet passed more quietly than the rest.

Two people were divinely happy, and two people supremely sad, and one mean little heart was full of bitterness, and malice unassuaged.

So after dinner was over, and they were all once more in the White Drawing-Room, the different elements assorted themselves.

Francis Markrute had taken his niece aside, to give her his bit of salutary information.

"We have all had a most delightful visit, I

am sure, Zara," he had said, "but you and Tristram seem not to be yet as good friends as I could wish."

He paused a moment, but, as usual, she did not speak, so he went on:

"There is one thing you might as well know. I believe you have not realised it yet, unless Tristram has told you of it himself."

She looked up now, startled; of what was she ignorant then?

"You may remember the afternoon I made the bargain with you about the marriage," Francis Markrute went on; "well, that afternoon Tristram had refused my offer of you and your fortune with scorn.

"He would never wed a rich woman, he said, or a woman he did not know or love, for any material gain, but I knew he would think differently when he had seen how beautiful and attractive you were, so I continued to make my plans. You know my methods, my dear niece."

Zara's blazing and yet pitiful eyes were all his answer.

"Well, I calculated rightly; he came to dinner that night, and fell madly in love with you, and at once asked to marry you himself, while he insisted upon your fortune being tied up entirely upon you, and any children that you might have, only allowing me to pay off the mortgages on Wrayth for himself.

"It would be impossible for a man to have

behaved more like a gentleman. I thought now, in case you had not grasped all this, you had better know."

And then he said anxiously:

"Zara, my dear child, what is the matter?" for her proud head had fallen forward on her breast, with a sudden deadly faintness, this indeed was the filling of her cup.

His voice pulled her together, and she sat up; and to the end of his life Francis Markrute will never like to remember the look in her eyes.

"And you let me marry him? You let me go on and spoil both our lives! What had I ever done to you, that you should be so cruel to me? Or is it to be revenged upon my mother, for the hurt she brought to your pride?"

"Zara," he said, anxiously, "tell me, what do you mean? I knew you never would consent to the bargain, unless you thought it was equal on both sides.

"I know your sense of honour, dear, but I calculated, and I thought rightly, that Tristram, being so in love with you, would soon undeceive you, directly you were alone.

"I never believed a woman could be so cold as to resist his wonderful charm. Zara, what has happened? Won't you tell me?"

But she sat there turned to stone. She had no thought to reproach him. Her heart and her spirit seemed broken, that was all.

"Zara, would you like me to do anything?

176

Can I explain anything to him? Can I help you to be happy? I assure you it hurts me awfully, if this will not turn out all right."

She rose a little unsteadily from her seat beside him.

"Zara, you cannot be indifferent to him forever, he is too splendid a man. Cannot I do anything for you?"

She looked at him, and her eyes in their deep tragedy seemed to burn out of her deadly white face.

"No, thank you, there is nothing to be done ... everything is too late now."

Then she added in the same monotonous voice.

"I am very tired: I think I will wish you a good-night."

With immense dignity she left him, and making her excuses with gentle grace to the Duke, and Lady Ethelrida, she glided from the room.

And Francis Markrute, as he watched her, felt his whole being wrung with emotion and pain.

"My God!" he said to himself. "She is a glorious woman, and it will, it must, come right, even yet."

* * *

People left by all sorts of trains and motors in the morning, but there were still one or two remaining, when the bride and bridegroom made their departure, in their beautiful new car, with its smart servants, which had come to fetch them, and take them to Wrayth.

Zara had taken the greatest pains to dress herself.

She remembered that Tristram had admired her the first evening they had arrived for this visit, when she had worn sapphire blue, so now she put on the same coloured velvet, and the sable coat, yes, he liked that best too, and she clasped some of his sapphire jewels in her ears, and at her throat.

No bride ever looked more beautiful or distinguished, with her flower-like complexion, and red burnished hair, all set off by the velvet and dark fur.

But Tristram, after the first glance, when she came down, never looked at her, he dared not. So they said their farewells quietly.

"Of course it must all come right, they look so beautiful!" Ethelrida exclaimed unconsciously, as she waved her last wave on the steps, as the motor glided away.

"Yes, it must indeed," whispered Francis, who was beside her, and she turned and looked into his face.

Of all the ordeals which Tristram had had to endure since his wedding, these occasions, upon which he had to sit close beside her in a motor, were the worst.

Fortunately, she liked plenty of windows open, and did not object to smoke, but with the new air of meekness which was on her face, nearly two hours with her, under a sable rug, was no laughing matter.

At the end of the first half hour of silence and nearness, her husband found he was obliged to concentrate his mind in order to prevent himself from clasping her in his arms.

So, until they got into his own county, the strained speechlessness continued, and then he looked out and said:

"We must have the car opened now, please smile and bow as we go through the villages."

So Zara leaned forward, when the footman had opened the landaulette top, and tried to look radiant, and every emotion convulsed her heart as they began to get near the park, with the village nestling close to its gates on the far side.

Presently they came through cheering yokels to the South Lodge, the furthest away from the village, under a triumphal arch of evergreens with banners floating, and mottoes of "God bless the Bride and Bridegroom," and "Health and long life to Lord and Lady Tancred."

Tristram now took her hand, and put his arm round her as they both stood up for a moment in the car, while he raised his hat and waved it gaily, and answered graciously:

"My friends, Lady Tancred and I thank you so heartily for your kind wishes, and your welcome home."

Then they sat down, and the car went on,

and his face became rigid again, and he let go her hand.

At the next arch by the bridge, the same thing, only more elaborately carried out, began again, for here were all the farmers of the hunt on horseback, of which Tristram was a great supporter.

The cheering and waving knew no end, and the cavalcade of mounted men followed them round outside the Norman tower, and to the great gates in the smaller one, where the portcullis had been.

All the village children were here, and the old women from the almshouses, and every wish for their happiness was shouted out.

They were both pale with excitement and emotion when they finally reached the hall door, in the ugly, modern Gothic wing, and were again greeted by all the household servants in rows.

And there was Michelham back at his master's old home, with a smart young groom of the chambers as second in command.

The stately Housekeeper in her black silk stepped forward, and in the name of herself and her subordinates bade the new mistress welcome, and hoped she was not fatigued, and presented her with a bouquet of white roses.

"His Lordship told us all, when he was here making the arrangements, that Your Ladyship was as beautiful as a white rose!"

Tears welled up in Zara's eyes, and her voice trembled, as she thanked them and tried to smile.

"She was quite overcome, the lovely young lady," they told one another after, "and no wonder. Any woman would be mad after His Lordship, it is quite to be understood."

How they all loved him, the poor bride thought! And he had told them she was a beautiful white rose, he felt like that about her then, and she had thrown it all away, and now he looked upon her with loathing and disdain.

Presently, he took her hand again, and placed it on his arm as they walked through the long corridor, and so to the splendid hall, with its stately staircase to the gallery above.

"I have prepared the state rooms for Your Ladyship, pending Your Ladyship's choice," Mrs Anglin said. "There is the boudoir, and the bed-room, and the bathroom, and His Lordship's dressing-room, all together, and I hope Your Ladyship will find them as handsome as we old servants of the family think they are!"

When they got to the enormous bed-room, with its windows looking out on the French garden and park, all in exquisite taste, furnished and decorated by the Adams themselves, Tristram gallantly bent and kissed her hand, as he said:

"I will wait for you in the boudoir, while you take off your coat, and Mrs Anglin will show you the toilet-service of gold, which was given by

Louis XIV, to a French grandmother, and which the Ladies Tancred always use when they are at Wrayth. I hope you won't find the brushes too hard."

He laughed and went out.

Zara, overcome with the state, and beauty and tradition of it all, sat down upon the sofa for a moment, to try to control her pain.

She was throbbing with rage and contempt at herself, at the remembrance that she, in her ignorance, her ridiculous ignorance, had insulted this man, this noble gentleman, who owned all these things, and had taunted him with taking her for her uncle's wealth!

How he must have loved her in the beginning, to have been willing to give her all this, after seeing her for only one night.

Tristram was standing by the window of the boudoir, when she went in, and Zara, who as yet knew very little of English things, admired the Adam style, and Mrs Anglin, leaving them discreetly for a moment, told him so timidly.

"Yes, it is rather nice," he said stiffly, and then went on:

"We shall have to go down now to this fearful lunch, but you had better take your sable boa with you, the great hall is so enormous, and all stone, it may be cold. I will get it for you."

He went back and found it on the chair. He brought it, and wrapped it round her casually, as

182

if she had been a stone, and then held the door for her to go out.

Zara's pride was stung, even though she knew he was doing exactly as she herself would have done.

Instead of the meek attitude she had unconsciously assumed for a moment, she walked beside him with her head in the air, to the admiration of Mrs Anglin, who watched them descend the stairs.

"She is as haughty-looking as our own Ladyship," she thought to herself. "I wonder how His Lordship likes that!"

The tables in the great hall were laid down each side, as in the olden time. The bride and bridegroom sat, with a principal tenant and his wife on either side of them, while the powdered footmen served them with lunch.

Presently the speeches began, and this was the most trying moment of all. For the land steward, who proposed their healths, said such nice things, and Zara realised how they all loved her lord, and her anger at herself grew and grew.

In each speech, from different tenants, there was some intimate friendly allusion about herself too, linking her always with Tristram, and these were the hints that hurt her the most.

Then Tristram rose to answer them, in his name and hers. And he made a splendid speech, and told them he had come back to live among them, and brought them a beautiful new lady.

Here he turned to her a moment and took and kissed her hand, he said he would always think of all their interests in every way, and look upon them as his dear old friends, and he and Lady Tancred would always endeavour to promote their welfare.

Then an old apple-cheeked farmer got up, and made a long rambling speech, about having been there, man and boy, and his forebears before him, for a matter of two hundred years, but he'd take his oath they had none of them ever seen such a beautiful bride brought to Wrayth as they were welcoming now!

He drank to Her Ladyship's health, and hoped it would not be long before they would have another and as great a feast for the rejoicings over the son and heir!

Tristram's resolve had held him; nothing could have been more gallingly cold and disdainful than had been his treatment of her, so perfect in its acting for "the game," and so bitter in the humiliation of the between times.

She would tell him of her mistake, and that was all, she must guard herself to show no emotion over it.

They each sank down into chairs beside the fire, with sighs of relief.

"Good Lord!" he said, as he put his hand to his forehead. "What a hideous mockery the whole thing is, and not half over yet.

"I am afraid you must be tired," he went on,

"you ought to go and rest until dinner. Please look very magnificent and wear some of the jewels, part of them have come down from London on purpose, I think, beyond those you had at Mont-fitchet."

"Yes, I will," she answered listlessly.

She began to pour out the tea, while he sat quite still, staring into the fire, a look of utter weariness and discouragement upon his handsome face.

She gave him his cup without a word. She had remembered, from Paris, his tastes in cream and sugar, and then, as the icy silence continued, she could bear it no longer.

"Tristram," she said, in as level a voice as she could, and at the sound of his name he looked at her, startled.

It was the first time she had ever used it!

She lowered her head, and clasping her hands she went on constrainedly, so overcome with emotion she dared not let herself go.

"I want to tell you something, and ask you to forgive me. I have learned the truth, that you did not marry me just for my uncle's money.

"I know exactly what really happened now. I am ashamed, humiliated, to remember what I said to you . . . but I understood you had agreed to the bargain before you had even seen me, and the whole thing seemed so awful to me, so revolting.

"I am sorry for what I taunted you with. I

185

know now that you are really a great gentleman."

His face, if she had looked up and seen it, had first lightened with hope and love, but as she went on coldly, the warmth died out of it, and a greater pain than ever filled his heart.

So she knew now, and yet she did not love him, there was no word of regret for the rest of her taunts, that he had been an animal, and the blow in his face! and the recollection of this suddenly lashed him again, and made him rise to his feet, all the pride of his race flooding his being once more.

He put down his tea-cup on the mantel-piece, and then he said hoarsely:

"I married you because I loved you, and no man has ever regretted a thing more."

Then he turned round and walked slowly from the room.

Zara, left alone, felt that the end had come.

* * *

A pale and most unhappy bride awaited her bridegroom in the boudoir at a few minutes to eight o'clock. She felt perfectly lifeless, as though she had hardly enough will left even to act her part.

The satin of her dress was as white as her face. The head gardener had sent up some splendid gardenias for her to wear, and the sight of them pained her, for were not these the flowers that Tristram had brought her that evening of her wedding day not a fortnight ago, and had then thrown into the grate?

Then, for her further unhappiness, she remembered that he had said:

"When the mockery of the rejoicings is over, then we can discuss our future plans."

What did that mean? That he wished to separate from her, she supposed. How could circumstances be so cruel to her? What had she done?

Tristram thought he had never seen her looking so un-English, so barbaric, that it suddenly filled him with wild excitement.

Could anything be more diabolically attractive, he thought, and for a second the idea flashed across him that he would seize her tonight and treat her as if she were the panther she looked, conquer her by force, beat her if necessary, and then kiss her to death!

But the training of hundreds of years of chivalry towards women and things weaker than himself was still in his blood. For Tristram, twenty-fourth Baron Tancred, was no brute or sensualist, but a very fine specimen of his fine old race.

"There is a stupid custom that I must kiss you as we go into the dining-room," he said, as they descended the staircase, "and give you this little golden key, a sort of ridiculous emblem of the 'endowment of all the wordly goods' business.

"The servants are, of course, looking at us, so please don't start."

Then he glanced up and saw the rows of interested, excited faces, and that devil-may-care
rollicking boyishness which made him so adored
came over him, and he laughed up at them, and
waved his hand, and Zara's rage turned to wild
excitement, too.

There would be the walk across the hall, and
then in sixty paces he would kiss her.

What would it be like? And in those sixty
paces her face grew more white while he came to
the resolve that for this one second he would yield
to temptation and not only brush her forehead
with his lips, as he had been his intention, but for
once, just for this once, he would kiss her mouth!

He was past caring about the footmen seeing.
It was his only chance!

When they came to the threshold of the big
double doors he bent down and drew her to him
and gave her the golden key, and then he pressed
his warm passionate lips to hers.

Oh! the mad joy of it, and even if it were
only from duty, and to play the game, she had not
resisted him, like she had before.

He felt suddenly absolutely intoxicated, as he
had on the wedding night. Why, why must this
ghastly barrier be between them? Was there nothing to be done?

Then he looked at his bride as they advanced
to the table, and he saw that she was so deadly
white, he thought she was going to faint, for in-

toxication affects people in different ways. For her the kiss had seemed the sweetness of death.

"Give Her Ladyship some champagne immediately," he ordered the butler, and still with shining eyes he looked at her, and said gently, "for we must drink our own healths."

But Zara never raised her lids, only he saw that her little nostrils were quivering, and by the rise and fall of her beautiful bosom he knew that her heart must be beating as madly as was his own, and a wild triumph filled him.

Whatever the emotion she was experiencing, whether it was anger or disdain, or one he did not care to hope for, it was a very strong one, she was not then so icily cold!

How he wished that there were some more ridiculous customs in his family! How he wished he might order the servants out of the room, and begin to make love to her all alone.

And just out of the devilment which was now in his blood, he took the greatest pleasure in "playing the game," and while the solemn footmen's watchful eyes were upon them he let himself go, and was charming to her, and then, each instance they were alone, he made himself freeze again so that she could not say he was not keeping to the bargain.

And thus, in wild excitement for them both, the dinner passed, and with her it was alternate torture and pleasure as well; but with him, for the first time since his wedding, there was not any pain.

* * *

The gardens at Wrayth were famous. The natural beauty of their position and the endless care of generations of loving owners had left them a monument of what nature can be trained into by human skill.

But November is not the time to judge of gardens, and Tristram wished the sun would come out. He waited for his bride at the foot of the staircase, and at eleven she came down.

He watched her as she put one slender foot before the other in her descent; he had not noticed before how ridiculously inadequate they were. Just little bits of baby feet, even in her thick walking boots.

She certainly knew how to dress, and adapt herself to the customs of a country; her short serge frock and astrakhan coat and hat were just the thing for the occasion, and she looked so attractive with her hands in her monster muff that he began to feel the pain again of longing for her, so he said icily:

"The sky is grey and horrid. You must not judge of things as you will see them today; it is all really rather nice in the summer."

"I am sure it is," she answered meekly.

They walked on in silence through the courtyard, and round under a deep arched doorway.

The beautiful garden stretched in front of

them. It was a most splendid and stately scene, even in the dull November gloom, with the groups of statuary, and the green turf, and the general look of Versailles.

"How beautiful it all is!" she said with bated breath, and clasped her hands in her muff. "And how wonderful to have the knowledge that your family has been here always, and these splendid things are their creation! I understand that you must be a very proud man."

"Yes, I suppose I am a proud man," he said, "but it is not much good to me; one becomes a cynic as one grows older."

Then, with casual indifference, he began to explain to her all about the gardens and their dates, as they walked along, just as though he were a rather bored host.

Zara's heart sank lower and lower, and she could not keep up her little plan to be gentle and sympathetic. She could not do more than say just "Yes" and "No" and presently they came through a door to the hothouses, and she had to be introduced to the head gardener, a Scotsman, and expressed her admiration of everything, and ate some wonderful grapes.

Tristram again "played the game" and chaffed and was jolly, and so they went out and through a clipped covered walk to another door in a wall, which opened onto the west side, the very old part of the house, and suddenly she saw the Italian parterre.

Each view as she came upon it she tried to identify with what she had seen in the pictures in *Country Life,* but things look so different in reality, with the atmospheric effects, from the cold grey of a print.

Only there was no mistake about this, the Italian parterre; and a sudden tightness grew round her heart, and she thought of Mirko and the day she had last seen him.

Tristram was startled into looking at her by a sudden catching of her breath, and to his amazement he perceived that her face was full of pain, as though she had revisited some scene connected with sorrowful memories.

There was even a slight drawing back in her attitude, as if she feared to go on and meet some ghost. What could it be? Then the malevolent sprite who was near him just now whispered:

"It is an Italian garden. She has seen such before in other lands, perhaps the man is an Italian, he looks dark enough."

So, instead of feeling solicitous and gentle with whatever caused her pain, he said, almost roughly:

"This seems to make you think of something, well, let us go on and get it over, and then you can go in!"

He would be no sympathetic companion for her sentimental musings over another man!

Her lips quivered for a moment and he saw

that he had struck home and was glad and grew more furious as he strode along. He would like to hurt her again if he could, for jealousy can turn an angel into a cruel fiend.

They walked on in silence, and a look, almost of fear, crept into her tragic eyes. She dreaded so to come upon Pan and his pipes. Yet, as they descended the stone steps, there he was in the far distance with his back to them, forever playing his weird music for the delight of all growing things.

She forgot Tristram, forgot she was passionately preoccupied with him, and passionately in love, forgot even that she was not alone.

She saw the firelight again, and the pitiful little figure of the poor little brother as he pored over the picture, pointing with his sensitive forefinger to Pan's shape.

Tristram, watching her, did not know what to think. For her face had become more purely white than usual, and her dark eyes were swimming with tears.

God! how she must have loved this man! In wild rage he stalked beside her until they came quite close to the statue.

Then he stepped forward with a sharp exclamation of annoyance, for the pipes of Pan had been broken, and lay there on the ground.

Who had done this thing?

When Zara saw the mutilation she gave a

piteous cry. To her, to the mystic part of her strange nature, this was an omen. Pan's music was gone, and Mirko, too, would play no more.

With a wail like a wounded animal, she slipped down on to the stone bench, and burying her face in her muff the tension of her soul of all these days broke down, and she wept bitter, anguished tears.

Tristram was dumbfounded.

He did not know what to do. Whatever the cause, it now hurt him horribly to see her weep, as if with a broken heart.

She sobbed and sobbed and clasped her hands, and Tristram could not bear it any longer.

"Zara!" he said, distractedly. "For God's sake, do not cry like this! What is it? Can I not help you?"

He sat down beside her and put his arm round her, and tried to draw her to him; he must comfort her, whatever her pain.

But she started up and ran from him; he was the cause of her forgetfulness.

"Do not!" she cried passionately. "Is it not enough for me to know that it is you, and thoughts of you, which have caused me to forget him! Go! I must be alone!"

And like a fawn she fled down one of the paths, and beyond a great yew hedge, and disappeared from view.

Tristram sat on the stone bench, too stunned to move. This was a confession from her then, he realised when his power to think came back to him. It was no longer surmise and suspicion, there *was* someone else.

Someone to whom she owed love, and he had caused her to forget him; and this thought made him stop his chain of reasoning abruptly. For what did that mean? Had he, then, after all, somehow made her feel, make her think of him?

Was this the secret in her strange mysterious face that drew him, and puzzled him always? Was there some war going on in her heart?

But the comforting idea which he had momentarily obtained from that inference of her words went from him, as he pondered, for nothing proved that her thoughts of him had been thoughts of love.

So, alternately trying to reason the thing out, and growing wild with passion and suspicion and pain, he at last went back to the house.

He expected he would have to go through the ordeal of luncheon alone, but as the silver gong sounded she came slowly down the stairs.

She made no apology or allusion to her outburst; she treated the incident as though it had never been! She held a letter in her hand, which had come by the second post, while they were out.

It was written by her uncle from London the night before, and contained his joyous news.

Tristram looked at her, and was again dumbfounded. She was certainly a most extraordinary woman!

And some of his rage died down, and he decided that, after all, he would not demand an explanation of her now, he would let the whole hideous rejoicings be finished first, and then in London he would sternly investigate the truth.

So, with stormy eyes, and forced calm, the pair sat down to luncheon, and Zara handed him the note she carried in her hand.

My Dear Niece,

I have to inform you of a piece of news that is a great gratification to myself, and I trust will cause you, too, some pleasure.

Lady Ethelrida Montfitchet has done me the honour to accept my proposal for her hand, and the Duke, her father, has kindly given his hearty consent to my marriage with his daughter, which is to take place as soon as things can be arranged with suitability.

I hope you and Tristram will arrive in time to accompany me to dinner at Glastonbury House, on Friday evening, where you can congratulate my beloved *fiancée*, who holds you in affectionate regard.

I am, my dear niece, always your devoted uncle,

Francis Markrute

"Good Lord!" Tristram exclaimed when he had finished reading it.

He had been so absorbed in his own affairs, he had never even noticed the financier's peregrinations.

"I expect they will be awfully happy! Ethelrida is such an unselfish, sensible, darling girl!"

And it hurt Zara, even in her present mood, for she felt the contrast to herself, in his unconscious tone.

"My uncle never does anything without having calculated it will turn out perfectly," she said bitterly; "only sometimes it can happen that he plays with the wrong pawns."

Tristram wondered what she meant. He and she had certainly been pawns in one of the Markrute games, and now he began to see this object, just as Zara had done.

Then the thought came to him. Why should he not ask her straight out now why she had married him? It was not from any desire for himself or his position, he knew that, but for what?

"You told me on Monday that you now knew the reason I had married you. May I ask you, why did you marry me?"

She clasped her hands convulsively; this brought it all back, her poor little brother, and she was not free yet from her promise to her uncle. She never failed to keep her word.

"Believe me, I had a strong reason, but I cannot tell it to you now."

And while the servants were handing the coffee, Zara rose, and making the excuse that she must write to her uncle at once, left the room to avoid further questioning.

Chapter
Seven

Tristram passed the afternoon outdoors, inspecting the stables, and among his own favourite haunts, and then rushed in too late for tea, and only just in time to catch the post.

He wrote a letter to Ethelrida, and his uncle-in-law, how ridiculous that sounded. He would be his uncle's and Zara's cousin by marriage!

Then, when he thought of dear Ethelrida, whom he had loved more than his own young sisters, he hurriedly wrote out, as well, a telegram of affection and congratulation, which he handed to Michelham as he came in to get the letters, and the old man left the room.

Then he remembered that he had addressed the telegram to Montfitchet, and Ethelrida would, of course, he now recollected, be at Glastonbury House, as she was coming up that day, so he went to the door and called out:

"Michelham, bring me back the telegram."

The grave servant, who was collecting all the

other letters from the post-box in the hall, returned and placed beside his master, on the table, a blue envelope.

Tristram hurriedly wrote out another, and handed it to the servant, who finally left the room.

Then he absently pulled out what appeared to be his original one, and glanced at it before tearing it up, and, before he realised what he did, his eye caught:

To Count Mimo Sykypri,
Immediately, tomorrow, wire me your news.
Cherisette

And his rage burst in a terrible oath, he noticed that stamps were enclosed. Then he threw the paper with violence into the fire!

There was not any more doubt or speculation; a woman did not sign herself Cherisette, little darling, except to a lover!

Cherisette! He was so mad with rage that, if she had come into the room at that moment, he would have strangled her there and then.

He forgot it was time to dress for dinner, forgot everything but his overmastering fury. He paced up and down the room, and then, after a while, his balance returned.

The law could give him no redress yet, she certainly had not been unfaithful to him in their brief married life, and the law reckons little of sins committed before the tie.

Nothing could come now of going to her, and reproaching her, only a public scandal and disgrace.

No, he must play his part until he could consult with Francis Markrute, learn all the truth, and then concoct some plan. Out of all the awful ruin of his life, he could at least save his name.

But Count Mimo Sykypri would get no telegram that night!

The idea that there could be any scandalous interpretations put upon any of her actions or words never even entered Zara's brain; so personally innocently unconscious was she of herself and her doings, that such a possible aspect of the case never struck her.

She was the last type of person to make a mystery, or in any way play a part. If she had ever so faintly dreamed that any doubts of her were troubling Tristram, she would have plainly told him the whole story, and chanced her uncle's wrath.

But she had not the slightest idea of it. She only knew that Tristram was stern and cold, and showed his disdain for her, and that even though she had made up her mind to be gentle and try to win him back with friendship, it was almost impossible.

She looked upon his increased icy contempt of her at dinner as a protest at her outburst of tears in the day.

So the meal was endured, and the moment the

coffee was brought he gulped it down, and then rose; he could not stand being alone with her for a moment.

She was looking so beautiful, and so meek, and so tragic. He could not contain the mixed emotions he felt, he only knew that if he had to bear them another minute he would go mad.

So, with hardly sufficient politeness, he said:

"I have some important documents to look over. I will wish you a good-night."

* * *

Zara could hardly contain her impatience to see if a telegram from Mimo had come for her in her absence. Tristram saw her look of anxiety and strain, and smiled grimly to himself.

She would get no answering telegram from her lover that day!

Worn out with the whole thing, Zara turned to him and asked if it would matter, or look unusual, if she said that she was so fatigued she would like to go to bed, and not have to come down to dinner.

Early after lunch on Friday, they started for London, planning to be at Park Lane at five.

No telegram had come for Zara, Mimo must be away, but in any case it showed that nothing unusual was happening, unless he had been called to Bournemouth by Mirko himself, and had left hurriedly.

This idea tortured her so, that by the time she

got to London she could not bear it, and felt she must go to Neville Street and see.

Francis Markrute was waiting for them in the library when they arrived. He seemed so full of the exuberance of happiness that she could not rush off until she had poured out, and pretended to enjoy, a lengthy tea.

At last, Zara was able to creep away. She watched for her chance, and with the cunning of desperation, finding the hall momentarily empty, stealthily stole out the front door.

But it was after half past six, and they were dining at Glastonbury House, in St. James's Square, at eight.

She got into a taxi quickly, finding one in Grosvenor Street, she was afraid to wait to look in Park Lane, in case, by chance, she should be observed, and at last she reached the Neville Street lodging, and rang the noisy bell.

The slatternly little servant said that the gentleman was "hout," but would the lady come in and wait: he would not be long, as he had said as how he was only going to take a telegram.

Zara entered at once.

A telegram, perhaps for her, yes, surely for her. She knew that there was no one else to whom Mimo would telegraph. She went up to the dingy attic studio.

A clock struck seven. Where could Mimo be? The minutes seemed to drag into an eternity. All sorts of possibilities struck her, and then she controlled herself and became calm.

There was a large photograph of her mother, which Mimo had coloured really well. It was in a silver frame upon the mantelpiece, and she gazed and gazed at that, and whispered aloud in the gloomy room:

"Maman, *adoree*, take care of your little one now, even if he must come to you soon."

The clock showed it was nearly half past seven. She could not wait another moment, and also she reasoned, if Mimo were sending her a telegram, it would be to Park Lane.

He knew she was coming up, she would get it there on her return, so she scribbled a line to Count Sykypri, and told him she had been, and why, and that she must hear at once, and then she left.

When she got back, it was twenty minutes to eight. Tristram was in the hall.

"Where have you been?" he demanded, with a pale stern face.

He was too angry and suspicious to let her pass in silence, and he noticed that her cheeks were flushed with nervous excitement.

"I cannot wait to tell you now," she panted. "And what right have you to speak to me in such a manner? Let me pass, or I shall be late."

"I do not care if you are late or not. You shall answer me!" he said furiously, barring the way.

"You bear my name, at all events, and I have a right, because of that, to know."

"Your name?" she said vaguely.

Then for the first time she grasped that there was some insulting doubt of her in his words.

She cast upon him a look of withering scorn, and with the air of an empress commanding an insubordinate guard, she flashed:

"Let me pass at once!"

But Tristram did not move, and for a second they glared at each other, and she took a step forward as if to force her way.

Then he seized her angrily in his arms. But at that moment Francis Markrute came out of his room, and Tristram let her go. With her head set haughtily she went on to her room.

"I see you have been quarrelling again," her uncle said, rather irritably, and then he laughed, as he went down. "I expect she will be late. Well, if she is not in the hall at five minutes to eight, I shall go in to dinner."

Tristram sat down upon the deep sofa, on the broad landing outside her room, and waited. The concentrated essence of all the rage and pain he had yet suffered seemed to be now in his heart.

But what had it meant, that look of superb scorn? She had no look of a guilty person.

At six minutes to eight she opened the door, and came in. She had simply flown into her clothes, in ten minutes!

Her eyes were still black as night, with resentment, and her bosom rose and fell, while in her white cheeks two scarlet spots flamed.

"I am ready," she said haughtily.

Not waiting for her husband, she swept on down the stairs exactly as her uncle opened the library door.

The dinner for Ethelrida's betrothal resembled in no way the one for Zara and Tristram, for except in those two hearts there was no bitter strain, and the *fiancée* in this case was radiantly happy, neither able nor caring to conceal their feelings.

The Dowager Lady Tancred arrived a few minutes after the party of three, and Zara heard her mother-in-law gasp as she said:

"Tristram, my dear boy!"

And then she controlled the astonishment in her voice, and went on more ordinarily, but still a little anxiously:

"I hope you are very well?"

So he was changed then to the eye of one who had not seen him since the wedding, and Zara glanced at him critically, and saw that, yes, he was indeed changed.

His face was perfectly set and stern, and he looked older. It was no wonder that his mother should be surprised.

Then Lady Tancred turned to Zara and kissed her.

"Welcome back, my dear daughter," she said.

Zara tried to answer something pleasant; above all things, this proud lady, who had so tenderly given her son's happiness into her keeping, must not guess how much there was amiss!

But Lady Tancred was no simpleton, she saw immediately that her son must have gone through much suffering and strain. What was the matter?

It tore her heart, but she knew him too well to say anything to him about it.

So she continued to talk agreeably to them, and Tristram made a great effort, and chaffed her, and became gay, and soon they went in to dinner.

While the ladies sipped their coffee in one of the drawing-rooms, Ethelrida drew Zara aside to talk to her alone.

"Zara," she said, taking her soft white hand, "I am so awfully happy with my dear love, that I want you to be so too; dearest Zara, won't you be friends with me now, real friends?"

Zara, won by her gentleness, pressed Ethelrida's hand with her other hand.

"I am so glad, nothing my uncle could have done would have given me so much pleasure," she said, with a break in her voice. "Yes, indeed, I will be friends with you, dear Ethelrida. I am so glad, and touched, that you should care to have me as your friend."

Francis Markrute was staying on to smoke a cigar with the Duke, and presumably say a snatched good-night to his *fiancée*, so Tristram was left to take Zara home alone.

Now he would be able to ask her to explain; but she outwitted him, for they no sooner got into the brougham, and he had just begun to speak, than she leaned back and interrupted him:

"You insinuated something on the stairs this evening, the vileness of which I hardly understood at first; I warn you I will hear no more upon the subject!"

Her voice broke suddenly, and she said passionately, and yet with a pitiful note:

"Ah! I am suffering so tonight . . . please . . . please, don't speak to me; leave me alone."

And Tristram was silenced.

Whatever it might be, she must explain soon, but he could not torture her tonight; and, in spite of his anger, and suspicions and pain, it hurt him to see her, when the lights flashed in upon them, huddled up in the corner, her eyes like a wounded deer's.

"Zara!" he said at last, quite gently. "What is the awful shadow that is hanging over you? If you will only tell me . . ."

But at that moment they arrived at the door, which was immediately opened, and she walked on, and then to the lift without answering, and entering, closed the door. For what could she say?

She could bear things no longer. Tristram evidently saw she had some secret trouble; she would get her uncle to release her from her promise, as far as her husband was concerned at least.

She hated mysteries, and if it had annoyed him for her to be out late she would tell him the truth, and about Mirko and everything.

Evidently he had been very angry, but this was the first time that he had even suggested that he had noticed she was troubled about anything, except that day in the garden at Wrayth.

Her motives were so perfectly innocent, that even now not the faintest idea dawned upon her that anything she had ever done could even look suspicious.

Tristram was angry with her because she was late, and had insinuated something out of jealousy, men were always jealous, she knew, even if they were perfectly indifferent to a woman.

What really troubled her terribly tonight was the telegram she found in her room.

It was from Mimo, saying Mirko was feverish again; really ill, he feared, this time.

Zara spent a night of anguish and prayer, little knowing what the morrow was to bring.

Tristram went out again to the Turf, and tried to divert his mind away from his troubles; there was no use in speculating any further, he must wait for an explanation, which he would not consent to put off beyond the next morning.

Zara got up and dressed early; she must be ready to go out, to try to see Mimo the moment she could slip away after breakfast.

She came down with her hat on; she wanted

to speak to her uncle alone, and Tristram, she thought, would not be there so early, only nine o'clock.

"This is energetic," Francis Markrute said, but she hardly answered him, and as soon as Turner and the footman had left the room she began at once:

"Tristram was very angry with me last night because I was out late. I had gone to obtain news of Mirko, I am very anxious about him, and I could give Tristram no explanation; I ask you to relieve me from my promise not to tell him about things."

The financier frowned: this was a most unfortunate moment to revive the family skeleton, but he was a very just man, and he saw directly that suspicion of any sort was too serious a thing to arouse in Tristram's mind.

"Very well," he said, "tell him what you think best, he looks desperately unhappy, you both do. Are you keeping him at arm's length all this time, Zara? Because, if so, you will lose him. You cannot treat a man of his spirit like that; he will leave you."

"I do not want to keep him at arm's length; he is there of his own will. I told you at Montfitchet, everything is too late. . . ."

Then the butler entered the room.

"Someone wishes to speak to Your Ladyship on the telephone, immediately," he said.

Zara forgot her usual dignity, as she rushed

across the hall to the library to talk. It was Mimo, of course, but her presence of mind came to her, and, as the butler held the door for her, she said:

"Call me a taxi at once."

She took the receiver up, and it was Mimo's voice, and in terrible distress.

It appeared, from his almost incoherent utterances, that Agatha had teased Mirko, and finally broken his violin. And that this had so excited him, in his feverish state, that it had driven him almost mad.

He had waited until all the household, including the nurse, were asleep, and crept from his bed, and dressed himself, and taking the money his Cherisette had given him, had arrived at his flat very early this morning, but he was so very ill, and could she come at once.

Tristram, entering the room at that moment, saw her agonised face, and heard her say:

"Yes, yes, dear Mimo, I will come now."

And before he could realise what she was doing, she brushed past him, and rushed from the room, and across the hall and into the waiting taxi-cab.

The name "Mimo" drove Tristram mad again. He stood for a moment deciding what to do, then he seized his coat and hat, and rushed out after her into Grosvenor Street.

Here he hailed another taxi, but hers was down beyond Park Street when he got into his.

"Follow that taxi!" he said to the driver.

"That green one in front of you; I will give you a sovereign if you never lose sight of it."

He must see. "Mimo!" the "Count Sykypri," to whom she had telegraphed! And she had the effrontery to talk to her lover in her uncle's house!

Tristram was so beside himself with rage that he knew that if he found them together he would kill her.

His taxi followed the green one, keeping it always in view. But as they followed it into a side street, a back tyre on his taxi went with a loud report, and the driver came to a stop.

Almost foaming with rage, Tristram saw the green taxi disappear round the further corner of a street, and he knew it would be lost to view before he could overtake it, and there was none other in sight.

He flung the man some money, and almost ran down the road; and when he turned the corner he could see the green taxi in the far distance, it was stopping at a door.

He had caught her then, after all; he could afford to go slowly now.

It was evidently a most disreputable neighbourhood, a sickening, nauseating revulsion crept over him. Zara, the beautiful, refined Zara, to be willing to meet a lover here! The brute was probably ill, and that was why she had looked so distressed.

He walked up and down rapidly twice, and

then he crossed the road, and rang the bell; the
taxi was still at the door. It was opened almost immediately by a maid.

He controlled his voice and asked politely to
be taken to the lady who had just gone in. With
a snivel of tears, Jenny asked him to follow her,
and while she was mounting in front of him, she
turned and said:

"It ain't no good, Doctor, I ken tell yer. My
mother was took just like that; and after she'd
once broke the vessel, she didn't live a hour."

"The doctor, missus," Jenny announced when
they reached the attic door, and Tristram entered
the room.

Zara was kneeling by a low iron bed, where
lay the little body of a child, who was evidently
dying.

Zara held his tiny hand, and the divine love
and sorrowful agony in her face wrung her husband's soul. A towel soaked with blood had fallen
to the floor.

Mimo, with his tall military figure shaking
with dry sobs, stood on the other side, and Zara
murmured, in a tender voice of anguish:

"My little one. My Mirko."

She was oblivious in her grief of any other
presence, and the dying child opened his eyes
and called faintly.

"Maman!"

Then Mimo saw Tristram by the door, and advanced with his finger on his quivering lips to meet him.

"Ah, sir," he said, "alas! you have come too late. My child is going to God!"

And all the manhood in Tristram's heart rose up in pity. Here was a tragedy too deep for human judgment, too deep for thoughts of vengeance, and without a word he turned and stole from the room.

As he stumbled down the dark, narrow stairs, he heard the sound of a violin, as it wailed out the beginning notes of the "Chanson Triste," and he shivered as if with cold.

When Tristram reached the street, he looked about him for a minute like a blinded man, and then, as his senses came back to him, his first thought was what he could do for her, that poor mother upstairs, with her dying child.

For that the boy was Zara's child he never doubted. Her child, and her lover's, had he not called her "Maman"?

So this was the awful tragedy in her life. He analysed nothing as yet, his whole being was paralysed with the shock, and the agony of it; the only clear thought he had was that he must help her, in whatever way he could.

The green taxi was still there, but he would not take it, in case she should want it. He walked on down the street, and found a cab for himself, and went to his old rooms in St James's Street.

The hall-porter was surprised to see him. Nothing was ready for His Lordship, but his wife would come up.

But Tristram required nothing, he wished to be alone.

Poor Zara, poor unhappy Zara! were his first thoughts, then he stiffened suddenly. This man must have been her lover before even her first marriage, for Francis Markrute had told him she had married very soon.

She was twenty-three years old now, and the child could not have been less than six; he must have been born when she was only seventeen!

What devilish passion in a man could have made him tempt a girl so young? Of course, this was her secret, and Francis Markrute knew nothing of it.

The sickening, sickening squalid tragedy of it all! And she, Zara, who had seemed so proud and so pure!

Her look of scorn only the night before at his jealous accusation came back to him. He could not remember a single movement or action of hers that had not been that of an untarnished queen.

What horrible actresses women were! His whole belief had crumbled to the dust.

The most terrible part of it all, to him, was the knowledge that, in spite of everything, he still loved her.

Loved her with a consuming, almighty passion, which he knew nothing now could kill. It had been put to the bitterest proof. Whatever she had done, he could love no other woman.

Then he realised that his life was over. The future a blank, unutterable hopeless grey, which must go on for years and years. For he could never come back to her again, not even to live in the house with her.

He must never see her again, or if once more, only for a business meeting, to settle things without scandal to either of them.

He would not go back to Park Lane for a week. He would give her time to see to the funeral without the extra pain of his presence.

The man had taken him for the doctor, and she had not even been aware of his entrance. He would go back to Wrayth alone, and there try to think out some plan.

He searched among the covered-up furniture for his writing-table, and found some paper, and sat down and wrote two notes, one to his mother.

He could not face her today, she must go without seeing him, but he knew his mother loved him, and in all deep moments never questioned his will, even if she did not understand it.

The note to her was very short, merely saying something was troubling him greatly, for the time, so neither he nor Zara would come to luncheon, and she was to trust him and not speak of this to anyone until he himself told her more.

He might come and see her in Cannes, the following week.

Then he wrote to Zara.

> I know everything. I understand now, and however I blame you for your deception of me, you have my deep sympathy in your grief.
>
> I am going away for a week, so you will not be distressed by seeing me. Then I must ask you to meet me, here or at your uncle's house, to arrange for our future separation.
>
> Yours,
> *Tancred*

He rang for a messenger boy, and gave him both notes, and picking up the telephone called up his valet, and told him to pack and bring his things here to his old rooms. And if Her Ladyship came in, to see that she immediately got the note he was sending round to her.

Francis Markrute would have gone to the City by now, and he was going to lunch with Ethelrida, so he telephoned to one of his clerks there, finding he was out for the moment, just to say he was called away for a week and would write later.

She should have the first words with her uncle. Whether she would tell him or not she must decide; he would not do anything to make her existence more difficult than it must naturally be.

And then, when all this was done, the passionate jealousy of a man overcame him again, and when he thought of Mimo he once more longed to kill.

❋ ❋ ❋

It was late in the afternoon when Zara got back to her uncle's house. She had been too distracted with grief to know or care about time, or what they would be thinking of her absence.

She would go to her uncle and let him help to settle things; she could count upon him to do that.

Francis Markrute, anxious and disturbed by Tristram's message, and her absence, met her as she came in, and drew her into the library.

The butler had handed her her husband's note, but she held it listlessly in her hand, without opening it. She was still too numb with sorrow to take notice of ordinary things.

Her uncle saw immediately that something terrible had happened.

"Zara, dear child," he said, and folded her in his arms, with affectionate kindness, "tell me everything."

She was past tears now, but her voice sounded strange.

"Mirko is dead, Uncle Francis," she said. "He ran away from Bournemouth because Agatha, the Morleys' child, broke his violin. He loved it, you know, especially as Maman had given it to him.

"He came in the night, all alone, ill with fever, to find his father, and he broke a blood-vessel

218

this morning, and died in my arms, in the poor lodging."

Francis Markrute had drawn her to the sofa now, and stroked her hands. He was deeply moved.

"My poor, dear child! My poor Zara!" he said.

"Oh, Uncle Francis, can't you forgive poor Mimo now? Maman is dead and Mirko is dead, and if you ever, someday, have a child yourself, you may know what this poor father is suffering. Won't you help us?

"He is always foolish, unpractical, he is distracted with grief. You are so strong, won't you see about the funeral for my little love?"

"Of course I will," he answered. "You must have no distresses. Leave everything to me."

He bent and kissed her white cheek, while he tenderly began to remove the pins from her fur toque.

"Thank you," she said gently, as she took the hat from his hand and laid it beside her. "I grieve because I loved him . . . my dear little brother. His soul was full of music, and there was no room for him here.

"And, oh! I loved Maman so! But I know that it is better as it is; he is safe there, with her now, far away from all his pain. He saw her when he was dying."

Then, after a pause, she went on:

"Uncle Francis, you love Ethelrida very

much, don't you? Try to look back and think how Maman loved Mimo, and he loved her. Think of all the sorrow of her life, and the great, great price she paid for her love; and then, when you see, try to be merciful."

Francis Markrute suddenly felt a lump in his throat. The whole pitiful memory of his beloved sister stabbed him, and extinguished the last remnant of rancour towards her lover, which had smouldered always in his proud heart.

There was a moisture in his clever eyes, and a tremulous note in his cold voice, as he answered his niece.

"Dear child, we will forget and forgive everything. My one thought about it all now is to do whatever will bring you comfort."

"Yes, there is one thing," she said, and there was the first look of life in her face.

"Mirko, when I last saw him at Bournemouth, played to me a wonderful air; he said Maman always came back to him in his dreams, when he was ill . . . feverish, you know . . . and that she had taught it to him.

"Will you send it to Vienna or Paris, to some great artist, and get it arranged, and then when I play it we shall always be able to see Maman?"

And the moisture gathered again in Francis Markrute's eyes.

"Oh, my dear!" he said. "Will you forgive me for my hardness, and my arrogance to you both?

I never knew, I never understood, until lately, what love could mean in life. And you, Zara, yourself, dear child, can nothing be done for you and Tristram?"

At the mention of her husband's name, Zara looked up, startled; and then a deeper tragedy than ever gathered in her eyes, as she rose.

"Let us speak of that no more, Uncle," she said. "Nothing can be done, because his love for me is dead. I killed it myself, in my ignorance. Nothing you or I can do is of any avail now; it is all too late."

Francis Markrute could not speak. Her ignorance had been his fault, his only mistake in calculation, because he had played with souls as pawns, in those days before love had softened him.

When she got to her room, she remembered that she still carried some note, and she at last looked at the envelope. It was in Tristram's writing.

In spite of her grief, and her numbness, it gave her a sharp emotion. She opened it quickly, and read its few cold words.

Then it seemed as if her knees gave way under her. She could not think clearly or fully understand their meaning; only one point stood out distinctly.

He must see her to arrange for their separation. He had grown to hate her so much, then, that he could no longer even live in the house with her, and all her grief of the day seemed less than this thought.

Then she read it again. He knew all? Who could have told him? Her Uncle Francis? No, he had not known himself that Mirko was dead until she told him. This was a mystery, but it was unimportant; her numb brain could not grasp it yet.

The main thing was that he was very angry with her for her deception of him; that, perhaps, was what was causing him finally to part from her. How strange it was that she was always punished for keeping her word, and acting up to her principles!

She did not think this bitterly, only with utter hopelessness.

There was no use her trying any longer, happiness was evidently not meant for her; she must just accept things, and life, or death, as it came. But how hard men were!

Then she felt her cheeks suddenly burn, and yet she shivered; and when her maid came to her presently she saw that her mistress was not only deeply grieved, but ill.

She put her quickly to bed, and then went down to see Mr Markrute.

"I think we must have a doctor, *Monsieur*," she said. "Milady is not at all well."

Francis Markrute, deeply distressed, telephoned at once for his physician.

For the four following days Zara lay in her

bed, seriously ill. She had caught a touch of influenza, the physician said, and had evidently had a most severe shock as well.

But she was naturally so splendidly healthy that, in spite of grief, and hopelessness, on the following Thursday she was able to get up again.

Francis Markrute thought that her illness had in a way been merciful, because the funeral had been got over while she was confined to her room.

It came to her as a comfort that her uncle and Mimo had met, and shaken hands in forgiveness, and now poor Mimo was coming to say good-bye to her that afternoon.

He was leaving England at once, and would return to his own country and his people. In his great grief, and with no future ties, he hoped they would receive him.

He had only one object now in life, to get through with it, and join those he loved, in some happier sphere.

Zara, in her weakness, had cried for a long time after he had left. Then she realised that all that part of her life was over now, and the outlook of what was to come held out no hope.

Francis Markrute had telegraphed to Wrayth to try to find Tristram, but he was not there. He had not gone there at all. At the last moment he could not face it, he felt; he must go somewhere away alone, by the sea.

A great storm was coming on, it suited his mood, so Tristram had left even his servant in

London, and had gone off to a wild place that he knew of on the Dorset coast, and there heard no news of anyone.

He would go back on Friday and see Zara the next day, as he had said he would do. Meanwhile, he must fight his ghosts alone. And what ghosts they were!

On Saturday morning Francis Markrute was obliged to leave his niece. His vast schemes required his attention in Berlin, and he would be gone a week, and then was going down to Montfitchet.

Ethelrida had written Zara the kindest letters. Her *fiancé* had told her all the pitiful story, and now she understood the tragedy in Zara's eyes, and loved her the more, for her silence and her honour.

And now that her health was better and she was able to think, she could not understand: How could Tristram possibly have known all? Had he followed her? As soon as she would be allowed to go out, she would go and see Jenny, and question her.

Tristram, by the wild sea, eventually came to some conclusions. He would return and see his wife, and tell her that now they must part, that he knew of her past, and he would trouble her no more.

He would not make her any reproaches, for of what use would they be? And, besides, she had suffered enough. Zara's week of separation from him had been grief and suffering, but his had been hell.

On Saturday morning, after her uncle had started for Dover, a note, sent by hand, was brought to Zara.

It was again only a few words, merely to say that if it was convenient to her, Tristram would come at two o'clock, as he was motoring down to Wrayth at three, and was leaving England on Monday morning.

Her hand trembled too much to write an answer.

"Tell the messenger I will be here," she said.

Then a thought came to her. Whether she was well enough or not, she must go and question Jenny.

So, to the despair of her maid, she wrapped herself in furs and started. She felt extremely faint when she got into the air, but her will pulled her through, and when she got there the little servant put her doubts at rest.

Yes, a very tall, handsome gentleman had come a few minutes after herself, and she had taken him up thinking he was the doctor.

So that was what had happened! Her thoughts were all in a maze, and she could not reason. When she got back to Park Lane she felt too feeble to go any further, even to the lift.

Her maid came and took her furs from her, and she lay on the library sofa, after Henriette had persuaded her to have a little chicken broth, and then she fell into a doze, and was awakened only by the sound of the electric bell.

She knew it was her husband coming, and sat up with a wildly beating heart. Her trembling limbs would not support her, as she rose for his entrance, and she held on by the back of a chair.

Grave and pale with the torture he had been through, Tristram came into the room. He stopped dead when he saw her so white and fragile-looking.

"Zara, you have been ill!" he exclaimed.

"Yes," she faltered.

"Why did they not tell me?" he said hurriedly, and then recollected himself; how could they? No one, not even his servant, knew where he had been.

She dropped back unsteadily to the sofa.

"Uncle Francis did telegraph to you, to Wrayth, but you were not there."

He bit his lips, he was so very moved. How was he to tell her all the things he had come to say so coldly, while she was looking so pitiful, so gentle?

His own longing was to take her to his heart, and comfort her, and make her forget all pain.

"Tristram," she said.

There was the most piteous appeal in her tones, which almost brought the tears to his eyes.

"Please . . . I know you are angry with me, for not telling you about Mirko and Mimo, but I had promised not to, and the poor little one is dead.

I will tell you everything presently, if you wish, but don't ask me to now.

"Oh! if you must go from me soon, you know best, I will not keep you, but . . . but please, won't you take me with you today back to Wrayth, just until I get quite well? My uncle is away, and I am so lonely, and I have no one else."

Her eyes had a pleading, frightened look, like a child who is afraid to be left alone in the dark.

He could not resist her. And, after all, her sin was of long ago, she could have done nothing since she had been his wife; why should she not come to Wrayth? She could stay there if she wished, for a while, after he had gone.

"Where is Count Sykypri?" he asked hoarsely.

"Mimo has gone away, back to his own country," she said simply, wondering at his tone. "Alas! I shall perhaps never see him again."

A petrifying sensation of astonishment crept over Tristram. With all her meek gentleness, she had still the attitude of a perfectly innocent person!

It must be because she was only half English, and foreigners perhaps had different points of reasoning on all such questions.

"Will you get ready now?" he said, controlling his voice into a note of sternness, which he was far from feeling. "Because I am sure you ought not to be out late in the damp air. I was going in the open car, and to drive myself, and it takes four hours. The closed one is not in London."

Then he saw she was not fit for this, so he said anxiously:

"But are you sure you ought to travel today at all? You look so awfully pale."

"Yes, yes, I am quite able to go," she said, rising to show him she was all right. "I will be ready in ten minutes. Henriette can come by train with my things."

She walked towards the door, which he held open for her. And here she paused, and then went on to the lift. He followed her quickly.

"Are you sure you can go up alone?" he asked anxiously, "Or may I come?"

"Indeed, I am quite well," she answered, with a little pathetic smile. "I will not trouble you. I shall not be long."

When she came down again, all wrapped in her furs, she found Tristram had port wine ready for her.

"You must drink a big glass of it," he said; and she took it without a word.

Then, when they got to the door, she found, instead of his own open motor, he had ordered one of her uncle's closed ones, which, with foot-warmer and cushions, was waiting, so that she should be comfortable, and not catch further cold.

"Thank you . . . that is kind of you," she said.

He helped her in, and the butler tucked the

fur rug over them, while Tristram settled the cushions. Then she leaned back for a second and closed her eyes; everything was going round.

She lay there back against the pillows, until they had got out of London. The wine, in her weak state, made her sleepy, and she gradually fell into a doze, and her head slipped sideways, and rested against Tristram's shoulder, and it gave him a tremendous thrill.

He was going to leave her so soon; and she would not know it, she was asleep. He must just hold her to him a little, she would be more comfortable like that.

So, with cautious care, not to awaken her, he slipped his arm under the cushion, and very gently and gradually drew her into his embrace, so that her unconscious head rested upon his breast.

He loved her so madly. What did it matter how she had sinned? She was ill and lonely, and must stay in his arms, just for today. But he could never really take her to his heart, the past was too terrible for that. And, besides, she did not love him; this gentleness was only because she was weak, and crushed for the time.

But how cruelly, bitterly sweet it was, all the same!

He had the most overpowering temptation to kiss her, but he resisted it, and presently, when they came to a level crossing, and a train gave a wild whistle, she woke with a start.

It was quite dark now, and she said in a frightened voice:

"Where am I? Where have I been?"

Tristram slipped his arm from round her instantly and turned on the light.

"You are in the motor, going to Wrayth," he said. "And I am glad to say you have been asleep. It will do you good."

She rubbed her eyes.

"Ah! I was dreaming. And Mirko was there too, with Maman, and we were so happy!" she said, as if to herself.

Tristram winced.

"Are we near home . . . I mean, Wrayth?" she asked.

"Not quite yet," he answered. "There will be another hour and a half."

"Need we have the light on?" she questioned. "It hurts my eyes."

He put it out, and they sat there in the growing darkness, and did not speak any more for some time: and, bending over her, he saw that she had dozed off again.

How very weak she must have been!

He longed to take her into his arms once more, but did not like to disturb her, she seemed to have fallen into a comfortable position among the pillows, so he watched over her tenderly, and presently they came to the lodge gates of Wrayth, and the stoppage caused her to wake and sit up.

"It seems I had not slept for so long," she

said, "and now I feel better. It is good of you to let me come with you. We are in the park, are we not?"

"Yes, we shall be at the door in a minute."

Then they arrived at the door, and this time they turned to the left before they got to the Adam's hall, and went down a corridor to the old panelled rooms, and into his own sitting-room, where it was warm and cosy, and the tea-things were laid out.

She already looked better for her sleep; some of the bluish transparency seemed to have left her face.

She had not been into this room on her inspection of the house. She liked it best of all, with its scent of burning logs, and good cigars. And Jake snorted by the fire, with pleasure to see his master, and she bent and patted his head.

But everything she did was filling Tristram with fresh bitterness and pain. To be so sweet and gentle now, when it was all too late!

He began opening his letters until the tea came.

There were the telegrams from Francis Markrute, sent a week before, to say Zara was ill, and many epistles from friends. And at the end of the pile, he found a short note from Francis Markrute as well.

It was written the day before, and said that he supposed he would get it eventually; that Zara had had a very sad bereavement, which he felt

sure she would rather tell him about herself,
and that he trusted, seeing how very sad and ill
she had been, that Tristram would be particularly
kind to her.

So her uncle knew, then! This was incredible.
But perhaps Zara had told him in her first grief.

He glanced up at her; she was lying back in a
great leather chair now, looking so fragile and
weary, he could not say what he intended.

Then Jake rose leisurely, and put his two fat
fore-paws upon her knees, and snorted, as was his
habit when he approved of anyone. And she bent
down and kissed his broad wrinkles.

It all looked so home-like and peaceful! Suddenly scorching tears came into Tristram's eyes,
and he abruptly rose and walked to the window.
And at that moment the servants brought the tea-
pot and the hot scones.

She poured the tea out silently, and then she
spoke a little to Jake, just a few silly, gentle
words, about his preference for cakes or toast.

She was being perfectly adorable, Tristram
thought, with her air of pensive, subdued sorrow,
and her clinging black dress. He wished she would
suggest going to her room. He could not bear it
much longer.

She wondered why he was so restless. And he
certainly was changed, he looked haggard and
unhappy, even more so than before.

Then she remembered how radiantly strong

and splendid he had appeared at dinner on their wedding night, and a lump rose in her throat.

"Henriette will have arrived by now," she said in a few minutes. "I will go to my room if you will tell me where it is."

He got up, and she followed him.

"I expect you will find it is the blue Chinese damask one, just at the top of these little stairs."

He strode on in front of her quickly, and called out from the top:

"Yes it is; and your maid is here."

As she came up the low, short steps, they met on the turn, and stopped.

"Good-night," he said. "I will have some soup, and suitable things for an invalid, sent up to you; and then you must sleep well, and not get up in the morning.

"I shall be very busy tomorrow. I have a great many things to do before I go on Monday. I am going away for a long time."

She held on to the bannisters for a minute, and the shadows were so deceiving, with all the black oak, that he was not sure what her expression said.

"Thank you . . . I will try to sleep. Good-night," she said softly.

Chapter
Eight

It was not until lunch-time that Zara came down the next day. She felt that he did not wish to see her, and she lay there in her pretty, old, quaint room and thought of the wreck their lives had become.

The thought of Tristram going tore her very soul, and swallowed up all other grief.

"I cannot . . . cannot bear it!" she moaned to herself.

He was sitting gazing into the fire when she timidly came into his sitting-room. She had been too unhappy to sleep much, and was again looking very pale.

He seemed to speak to her like one in a dream; he was numb with his growing misery, and the struggle in his mind.

He must leave her, the situation was unendurable, he could not stay, because in her present softened mood, it was possible that, if he lost control of himself and caressed her, she might yield to him; and then he knew no resolution on earth could hold him from taking her to his heart.

She must never really be his wife. The bliss of it might be all that was divine at first, but there would be always the hideous skeleton beneath, ready to peep out and mock at them.

He never once looked at her, and spoke as coldly as ice; and they got through luncheon.

Zara said suddenly she would like to go to church. It was at three o'clock, so he ordered the motor without a word. She was not well enough to walk there through the park.

He could not let her go alone, so he changed his plans and went with her. They did not speak all the way.

She had never been into the church before, and was struck with the fine windows, and the monuments of the Guiscards. And a wild, miserable rebellion filled her heart, and then a cold fear, and she passionately prayed to God to protect Tristram.

For what if he should go on some dangerous hunting expedition, and she should never see him again! And then, as she stood while they sang the final hymn, she stopped and caught her breath with a sob.

Tristram glanced at her in apprehension, and he wondered if he should have to suffer anything further or if his misery was at its height.

Zara went to her room when they got back to

the house, and when she came down to tea he was not there, and she had hers alone with Jake.

She felt almost afraid to go to dinner. It was so evident he was avoiding her. And while she stood undecided, her maid brought in a note:

I ask you not to come down, I cannot bear it. I will see you tomorrow morning before I go, if you will come to my sitting-room at twelve.

She used the whole strength of her will to control herself the next morning. She must not show any emotion, no matter how she should feel.

It was not that she had any pride left, or would not have willingly fallen into his arms; but she felt no woman could do so unsolicited, and when a man plainly showed her that he held her in disdain.

"I have only ten minutes," he said constrainedly. "The motor is at the door. I am going round by Bury St Edmunds; it is an hour out of my way, and I must be in London at five o'clock, as I leave for Paris by the night mail. Will you sit down, please, and I will be as brief as I can."

She fell, rather than sank, into a chair. She felt a ringing in her ears; she must not faint, she was so very weak from her recent illness.

"I have arranged that you stay here at Wrayth until you care to make fresh arrangements for yourself," he began, averting his eyes, and speaking in a cold, passionless voice.

"But if I can help it, when I leave here today, I will never see you again. There need be no public scandal; it is unnecessary that people should be told anything, they can think what they like.

"I will explain to my mother that the marriage was a mistake and we have agreed to part, that is all.

"You can live as you please, and I will do the same. I do not reproach you for the ruin you have brought upon my life. It was my own fault for marrying you so heedlessly. But I loved you so. . . ."

His voice broke suddenly, and he stretched out his arms wildly.

"My God!" he cried. "I am punished! The agony of it is that I love you still, with all my soul, even though I saw them with my own eyes . . . your lover and . . . your child!"

Zara gave a stifled shriek, and as he strode from the room, not daring to look at her, for fear of breaking his resolution, she rose unsteadily to her feet, and tried to call him.

But she gasped, and no words would come. Then she fell back unconscious in the chair.

He did not turn round, and soon he was in the motor and gliding away as though the hounds of hell were after him, as indeed they were, from the mad pain in his heart.

When Zara came to herself, it was half an

hour later, and he was many miles away. She sat up, and found Jake licking her hands.

Then remembrance came back. He was gone, and he loved her, even though he thought her . . . that!

She started to her feet. The blood rushed back to her brain. She must act.

She stared round, dazed for a moment, and then she saw the timetables, the Bradshaw and the ABC. She turned over the leaves of the latter with feverish haste.

Yes, there was a train which left at two-thirty, and got to London at half past five.

Then she put her hand to her head in agony. She did not know where he had gone. Would he go to his mother's, or to his old rooms in St. James's Street? She did not know their number. She rang the bell and asked that Michelham should come to her.

The old servant saw her ghastly face, and knew from Higgins that his master intended going to Paris that night.

He guessed some tragedy had happened between them, and longed to help.

"Michelham," she said, "His Lordship has gone to London. Do you know to what address? I must follow him; it is a matter of life and death that I see him before he starts for Paris. Order my motor for the two-thirty train; it is quicker than to go by car all the way."

"Yes, My Lady," Michelham said. "Everything will be ready. His Lordship has gone to his rooms, 460 St. James's Street. May I accompany Your Ladyship? His Lordship would not like Your Ladyship to travel alone."

"Very well," she said. "There is no place anywhere within driving distance that I could catch a train that got in before, is there?"

"No, My Lady; that will be the quickest," he said. "And will Your Ladyship please eat some luncheon? There is an hour before the motor will be round."

"Yes, yes, Michelham," said Zara, and hurried from the room.

She sent a telegram when at last she reached the station, to the St. James's Street rooms.

What you thought was not true, do not leave
until I come and explain. I am your own.
                                        Zara

Then the journey began, three hours of agony, with the constant stoppages, and the one thought going over and over in her brain. He believed she had a lover and a child, and yet he loved her!

Oh God, that was love indeed, and she might not be in time. But at last they arrived, and drove to Tristram's rooms.

Yes, His Lordship had been expected at five,

but had not arrived yet, he was late. And Michelham explained that Lady Tancred had come and would wait, while he himself went round to Park Lane to see if Lord Tancred had been there.

He made up a splendid fire in the sitting-room, and, telling Higgins not to go in and disturb her, even with tea, the kind old man started on his quest, much anxiety in his mind.

The minutes passed, and Zara felt she could hardly bear the suspense. The mad excitement had kept her up until now. What if he were so late that he went straight to the train? But then she remembered it went at nine, and it was only six. Yes, he would surely come.

She had seen two or three telegrams lying on the little hall table waiting for him, as she came in, hers among them, she supposed.

It was hot in the room and she took off her hat and coat. Her hair glistened in the light of the flames but after a while she felt cold with fear.

Suddenly she heard a motor stop outside.

She sat still, her heart beating in her throat. There was the sound of a latch-key turning in the lock! And, after stopping to pick up his telegrams, Tristram entered the room.

She rose unsteadily to meet him, and he gave an exclamation of surprise and pain.

"Tristram!" she faltered.

It seemed as if her voice had gone again, and the words would make no sound. But she gathered her strength and with pitiful pleading stretched out her arms.

"Tristram, I have come to tell you . . . I have never had a lover; Mimo was at last married to Maman, he was her lover, and Marko was their child . . . my little brother. My uncle did not wish me to . . . tell you this for a time, because it was the . . . family disgrace."

He gave an exclamation and stepped towards her with an expression of passionate joy in his face as she went on:

"Tristram, you said that night . . . before you would ever ask me to be your wife again I must go down upon my knees. . . . See, I am there . . . on my knees . . . for, oh . . . I love you!"

She knelt before him, and bowed her proud head.

But she did not stay in this position more than a moment, for he lifted her to clasp her passionately in his arms. He rained wild triumphant kisses upon her beautiful curved lips, while he murmured:

"At last—my love—my own!"

* * *

When the delirium of joy had subsided a little, he tenderly drew her to the sofa before the fire!

It was an inexpressible happiness to feel her resting against him unresisting, with her eyes, which had been so stormy and resentful, now melting in soft passion.

It seemed heaven to them both. They could not speak coherent sentences for a while, and over and over again they told each other, "I love you ... I love you."

It seemed as if Tristram could not hear her sweet confession often enough, or quench the thirst of his parched soul upon her lips.

Then the masterfulness in him, which Zara now adored, asserted itself. He must play with her hair! He must undo it, and caress its waves, to blot out all remembrances of how its forbidden beauty had tortured him.

And she just lay there in his arms, in one of her silences, only her eyes were slumbrous with love.

But at last she said; nestling closer:

"Tristram, won't you listen to the story that I must tell you? I want there never to be any more mysteries between us again."

And to content her he brought himself back to earth.

"Only, I warn you, my darling," he said, "all such things are unimportant for me now that at last we have found the only thing which really matters in life.

"We know that we love each other, and are not going to be so foolish as to part again, for a single hour if we can help it, for the rest of time."

His whole face lit up with radiant joy, and he suddenly buried it in her hair.

"See," he murmured, "I am to be allowed to

play with this exquisite net to ensnare my heart, and you are not to be allowed to spend hours in State Rooms, alone!"

"Oh! darling! how can I listen to anything but the music of your voice, when you tell me you love me, and are my very own!"

However, Zara did finally get him to understand the whole history, from beginning to end.

He heard of her unhappy life, and her mother's tragic story and her sorrow and poverty, and her final reason for agreeing to the marriage.

She told what she had thought of men, and then of him, and her gradual awakening into this great love.

He listened with a reverent tenderness.

"Oh! my sweet, my sweet," he said, "and I dared to be suspicious of you, and doubt you, it seems incredible now!"

Then he had to tell his story of how reasonable his suspicions looked, and in spite of them of his increasing love.

"And to think, Tristram, my darling husband," said Zara, "a little common sense would have smoothed it all out."

"No, it was not that," he answered proudly, with a whimsical smile in his eye; "the troubles would never have happened at all, if I had only not paid the least attention to your haughty words in Paris, or even at Dover, but had just continued making love to you, all would have been well!"

He kissed her wildly as if to make up for the time they had lost.

"However," he added joyously, "we will forget dark things, because tomorrow I shall take you back to Wrayth, and we shall have our real honeymoon there in perfect peace."

As her lips met his Zara whispered softly once again: "I love you ... I love you."

* * *

Oh! the glorious joy of that second homecoming for the bridal pair! To take walks to all Tristram's favourite haunts, to wander in the old rooms and plan out their improvements. And in the late afternoons to sit in the firelight in his own sitting-room, and make pictures of their future together.

His passionate delight in her seemed as if it could not find enough expression, as he grew to know the cultivation of her mind and the pure thoughts of her soul.

Her tenderness to him was all the sweeter in its exquisite submission, because her general mien was so proud.

And when they went to Montfitchet again for Christmas, the old Duke was satisfied!

* * *

All this happened two years ago. And on the second anniversary of the Tancred wedding, Mr Francis and Lady Ethelrida dined with their nephew and niece.

When they came to drinking healths, bowing to Zara, her uncle raised his glass and said:

"I propose a toast that I prophesied I would to you, my very dearest, beautiful niece, the toast of four supremely happy people!"

And as they drank, the four joined hands.

ABOUT THE EDITOR

BARBARA CARTLAND, the celebrated romantic author, historian, playwright, lecturer, political speaker and television personality, has now written over 150 books. Miss Cartland has had a number of historical books published and several biographical ones, including that of her brother, Major Ronald Cartland, who was the first Member of Parliament to be killed in the War. This book had a Foreword by Sir Winston Churchill.

In private life, Barbara Cartland, who is a Dame of the Order of St. John of Jerusalem, has fought for better conditions and salaries for Midwives and nurses. As President of the Royal College of Midwives (Hertfordshire Branch), she has been invested with the first Badge of Office ever given in Great Britain, which was subscribed to by the Midwives themselves. She has also championed the cause for old people and founded the first Romany Gypsy Camp in the world.

Barbara Cartland is deeply interested in Vitamin Therapy and is President of the British National Association for Health.

Introducing...
Barbara Cartland's
Library of Love

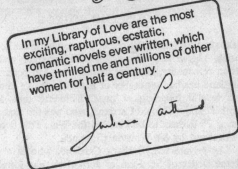

In my Library of Love are the most exciting, rapturous, ecstatic, romantic novels ever written, which have thrilled me and millions of other women for half a century.

Barbara Cartland

The World's Great Stories of Romance Specially Abridged by Barbara Cartland For Today's Readers.

☐	THE WAY OF AN EAGLE by Ethel M. Dell	10927	$1.50
☐	THE REASON WHY by Elinor Glyn	10926	$1.50
☐	THE HUNDREDTH CHANCE by Ethel M. Dell	10925	$1.50
☐	THE KNAVE OF DIAMONDS by Ethel M. Dell	10527	$1.50
☐	A SAFETY MATCH by Ian Hay	10506	$1.50
☐	HIS HOUR by Elinor Glyn	10498	$1.50
☐	THE SHEIK by E. M. Hull	10497	$1.50

Buy them at your local bookstore or use this handy coupon: